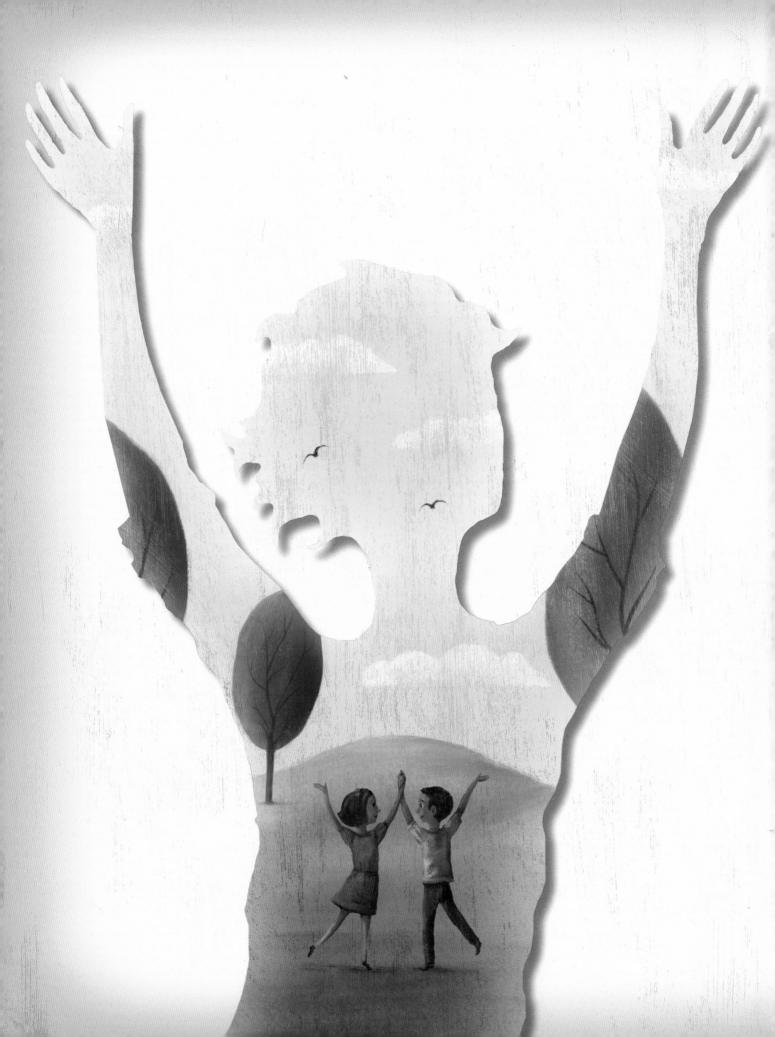

BELIEVE
STORYBOOK

Think, Act, Be Like Jesus

WRITTEN BY
RANDY FRAZEE
WITH
LAURIE LAZZARO KNOWLTON

ILLUSTRATED BY
STEVE ADAMS

Dedicated to Ava & Crew. Nana and BaBa taught this to your
mom and now we pass it on to you with love.

—RF

To our Christ, who gifted me with my talent; to my parents, Patrick
and Charlotte, who encouraged me; and to Barbara Herndon, who
provided me with the great opportunity to share the Word.

—LLN

In memory of my father, Raynald, who inspired
me throughout this great journey.

—SA

ZONDERKIDZ

Believe Storybook
Text copyright © 2015 by Randy Frazee
Bible stories copyright © 2015 by Laurie Lazzaro Knowlton
Illustrations copyright © 2015 by Steve Adams

Requests for information should be addressed to:

Zonderkidz, 3900 *Sparks Drive SE, Grand Rapids, Michigan 49546*

The Library of Congress has cataloged the printed edition as follows:
Frazee, Randy, author.
        Believe storybook: think, act, be like Jesus / by Randy Frazee with Laurie
Lazzaro Knowlton.
            pages   cm
        Summary: "Presented by author and pastor Randy Frazee, *The Believe*
storybook shows children 4-8 how they can think, act, and be more like
Jesus with 60 stories from the Bible that showcase the themes."
        Audience: Ages 4-8
        ISBN 978-0-310-74590-7 (hardcover)
        1. Christian children—Conduct of life—Juvenile literature. 2. Christian
children— Religious life—Juvenile literature. 3. Bible stories, English. [1. Conduct
of life.] I. Knowlton, Laurie Lazzaro, author. II. Title.
BV4571.3F73 2015
268'.8'2—dc23   2014031682

Contributor: Glenys Nellist
Editor: Barbara Herndon
Art direction/design: Cindy Davis

Printed in China

15 16 17 18 19 /DSC/ 11 10 9 8 7 6 5 4 3 2 1

Table of Contents

THINK

Chapter 1: GOD
God's Wonderful Creation..13
The Baptism of Jesus...16

Chapter 2: PERSONAL GOD
The Lord Is My Shepherd..21
Why Worry?...25

Chapter 3: SALVATION
Adam and Eve Disobey God...29
He Has Risen!..33

Chapter 4: THE BIBLE
Rules to Live By...37
Jesus Is Tempted...40

Chapter 5: IDENTITY IN CHRIST
God Changes Abram's and Sarai's Names..45
The Change in Zacchaeus..48

Chapter 6: CHURCH
God Builds a Nation..53
The Holy Spirit Comes to Establish the Church..56

Chapter 7: HUMANITY
Cain and Abel..61
The Lost Sheep Is Found..64

Chapter 8: COMPASSION
Ruth and Boaz..69
The Good Samaritan...73

Chapter 9: STEWARDSHIP
Hannah and Samuel..77
A Widow's Gift...81

Chapter 10: ETERNITY
Elijah Goes to Heaven..85
John's Vision of Heaven..88

ACT

Chapter 11: WORSHIP
Daniel Only Worships God 95
Paul and Silas Worship God in Prison 99

Chapter 12: PRAYER
Gideon Talks to God 103
Jesus Teaches His Disciples to Pray 107

Chapter 13: BIBLE STUDY
God Tells Joshua to Remember the Law 111
Jesus Teaches about Four Kinds of Soil 115

Chapter 14: SINGLE-MINDEDNESS
Jehoshaphat Prays to God for Help 119
Jesus Walks on Water 123

Chapter 15: TOTAL SURRENDER
The Fiery Furnace 127
Stephen's Story 131

Chapter 16: BIBLICAL COMMUNITY
Rebuilding the Wall of Jerusalem 135
A Community of Believers 139

Chapter 17: SPIRITUAL GIFTS
Daniel Interprets the King's Dream 143
Peter Heals a Crippled Man 147

Chapter 18: OFFERING MY TIME
God's People Finish Building the Temple 151
Jesus in His Father's House 155

Chapter 19: GIVING MY RESOURCES
Gifts for the Tabernacle 159
The Wise Men Visit Jesus 162

Chapter 20: SHARING MY FAITH
Jonah Tells Other People about God 167
Philip Shares the Bible with a Man from Ethiopia 171

BE

Chapter 21: LOVE
David and Jonathan 177
A Good Shepherd Loves His Sheep 181

Chapter 22: JOY
Celebrating the Joy of the Lord 185
Angels Give the Shepherds Joyful News 188

Chapter 23: PEACE
Solomon's Kingdom at Peace 193
Jesus Calms the Storm 197

Chapter 24: SELF-CONTROL
Samson Loses Control 201
The Lost Son 205

Chapter 25: HOPE
Isaiah the Prophet Brings Hope 209
Simeon's Story 212

Chapter 26: PATIENCE
David's Patience with King Saul 217
Jesus Heals a Disabled Man 221

Chapter 27: KINDNESS/GOODNESS
David Shows Kindness to Jonathan's Son 225
Jesus Talks about Kindness 228

Chapter 28: FAITHFULNESS
God and Joseph: Faithful to One Another 233
The Angel's Visit 237

Chapter 29: GENTLENESS
Abigail Is Gentle with David 241
Jesus Gently Questions Peter 245

Chapter 30: HUMILITY
God Humbles a Proud King 249
Jesus Humbles Himself in Front of His Disciples 253

Believe is unlike any other children's Bible storybook. It explores some of the greatest themes of the Bible—such as love, hope, forgiveness, and purpose. Instead of beginning with Genesis and ending with Revelation, this innovative storybook begins with the greatness of God and ends with the humility of Jesus. In between, children will encounter all their favorite Bible characters and beloved Bible stories.

Throughout the pages of *Believe*, you and your child will explore some of life's biggest questions such as: Who is God? How do I keep my focus on Jesus? How do I deal with the hardships and struggles of life? *Believe* then sets out to find the answers, with the aim of encouraging your child to *Think*, *Act*, and *Be* like Jesus.

Following the same pattern as the adult book, the first ten chapters of *Believe* outline the core *Beliefs* of Christian life. Together they answer the question, "What do I believe?" This section explores how we might *Think* like Jesus.

The second ten chapters discuss the core *Practices* of Christian life. Together they answer the question, "What should I do?" In other words, how can we *Act* like Jesus?

The final ten chapters contain the core *Virtues* of Christian life. Together they answer the question, "Who am I becoming?" The focus here is on how we might *Be* like Jesus.

Each of the thirty chapters in *Believe* begins by asking *The Key Question* and then sets out to find the answers in Scripture. One Old Testament story and one New Testament story are linked together around a common theme, while *The Jump to Jesus* provides the bridge between the two stories. *The Jesus Answer* helps you and your child discover how Jesus would answer the key question.

As you turn the page with your children and read the first core belief about God himself, remember *Believe* is an action word. God is personally watching over you as you embark on this journey together. He doesn't want your children to just believe these truths in their heads; he wants them to believe his Word with their whole hearts and make it the operating system for their lives. He wants to transform their lives for good and forever. He wants to put the "extra" in your "ordinary" so you and your family can live an "extraordinary" life in Christ—if you just BELIEVE.

Father, you fully know the children who hold this book in their hands. You know them by name. You love them deeply—always have, always will. As they embark on this amazing journey, as they look at the pictures and hear your Word, give them the faith to believe your truths with their whole heart. Do a work within them. Let that good work push out of their mouths, ears, hands, and feet to impact them as they grow and positively affect the people you will place around them. As they finish reading the last page, may they whisper to you and then shout to the world—I BELIEVE!

THINK
LIKE
JESUS

CHAPTER 1

God

THINK

The Key Question: Who is God?

Wow! What a big question! When you close your eyes, what picture of God do you see? Who do you think God is?

Do you think God is a big, strong daddy who takes care of you? He is!

Do you think God is Jesus, who loves you more than anything in the whole world? He is!

Or do you think God is invisible, like the wind, whispering into your heart? He is!

> *He's a daddy (that's the Father).*
> *He's Jesus (that's the Son).*
> *And he's an invisible wind (that's the Holy Spirit).*

There's no one like our great God. Let's find out more about God as we start at the very beginning ...

God's Wonderful Creation

Genesis 1–2

In the very beginning of time, God decided to create the world. On the first day of creation, God separated light from darkness. "The light will be called 'day' and the darkness 'night,'" God said.

On the second day, God said, "The waters need to divide." So he separated the sky above from the world below.

On the third day, God saw the earth covered with water. "This earth needs dry land," he said. Then he rolled back the waters so dry ground appeared. God said, "Let plants and towering trees grow." And beautiful gardens grew and filled the world with color.

"We need a source of light for the day and night," God said. So he rolled up a ball of warm colors and formed a sun. God painted the night sky with sparkling stars and a bright moon. This was a beautiful fourth day.

On day five, God sprinkled the seas with colorful, swimming fish. The gentle breeze sang the songs of birds in flight. God loved his creation.

On day six, God said, "Let all sorts of animals fill the earth." So he created lions, giraffes, elephants, and frogs. Bunnies hopped, kitties meowed, and dogs barked *bow-wow*!

"Something is still missing," God said. From the earth, he made a man and then a woman. "I give you all that you see," he told them. "Take care of my creation. Be good to each other. Fill your home with children and happiness." God watched the sun set on the sixth day.

When the sun rose on the seventh day, God declared, "Today is a day of rest!" And he smiled at all he had created.

The Jump to Jesus

Everything begins with God. He created all things—from the biggest to the smallest, from the anthill to the mountain, from the bee to the buffalo, from parents to little people, like you! Now wouldn't you think that the whole world would want to trust and obey such a wonderful God? But the Bible tells us that God's people did not do that! They forgot about God. They disobeyed him.

So God sent Jesus—his precious, only Son so that he could remind people to choose God again. And when Jesus came, he helped to answer the question about who God really is. As you read this story about when Jesus was baptized, see if you can spot the three persons of God … the Father, the Son, and the Holy Spirit.

The Baptism of Jesus
Luke 3

Jesus had a cousin named John who lived in the desert. John wore animal skins. When he was hungry, he ate bugs and honey. God had a special job for John. God said, "You will be my messenger. Tell the people to get ready for God to come to earth."

So John preached loudly to the people. He said, "You need to be sorry for your sins! Start obeying God's laws!"

Many people came from the cities and villages to hear John speak about the Messiah, the Savior who was coming. The people knew John spoke the truth. They said, "We are sorry for our sins."

Then John baptized the people in the Jordan River. He said, "I have baptized you with water. He will baptize you with the Holy Spirit."

The people celebrated being washed clean of their sins. They were now members of God's family.

One day, Jesus came to John at the Jordan River. John did not feel worthy to baptize Jesus. "I need to be baptized by *you*. Why are you coming to *me*?" John said this because Jesus had never sinned.

Jesus explained, "This is what God wants us to do."

Like the other people, Jesus went into the water, and John baptized him. Then a great light shone from the sky. The Holy Spirit came down on Jesus like a dove. A voice from heaven said, "This is my own dear Son, with whom I am pleased."

THE JESUS ANSWER

Did you spot the three different persons of God in that story? God the Father spoke from heaven, Jesus the Son was baptized, and the Holy Spirit came down like a dove.

Just like the three persons of God were there when Jesus was baptized, they are with us every day too. The Holy Spirit helps us see who God really is. God the Father is our creator, the one true, powerful God, who wants us to choose him above everything else. And Jesus came to show us how to do just that.

Do you believe in the one true God? If you believe this, you will be choosing the most wonderful life of all—because you will belong to him.

Believe!

KEY IDEA:

I believe the God of the Bible is the only true God—Father, Son, and Holy Spirit.

KEY VERSE:

May the love that God has given us be with you.

—2 Corinthians 13:14

CHAPTER 2

Personal God

THINK

The Key Question:
Does God Care About Me?

Of course our one true, powerful God cares about you. But how do you know for sure? You can know that God cares about you because the Bible tells us so.

The Bible is full of true stories about real people just like you and me—boys and girls, moms and dads, grandmas and grandpas—who knew God, talked to God, and found out just how much he really does care. And one of those people was a little shepherd boy called David …

The Lord Is My Shepherd
Psalm 23

David wrote many psalms to God. Psalms are poems or songs. David sang many of the psalms. In this psalm, David is showing God's love and care for us. David speaks of God as a shepherd and of himself as one of the shepherd's beloved sheep.

The LORD is my shepherd. He gives me everything I need.

He lets me lie down in fields of green grass.

He leads me beside quiet waters.

He gives me new strength.

He guides me in the right paths

for the honor of his name.

Even though I walk

through the darkest valley,

I will not be afraid.

You are with me.

Your shepherd's rod and staff

comfort me.

You prepare a feast for me
right in front of my enemies.
You pour oil on my head.
My cup runs over.

I am sure that your goodness and love will follow me
all the days of my life.
And I will live in the house of the LORD
forever.

The Jump to Jesus

What a beautiful psalm David wrote. But the most beautiful part of all is that God is *your* shepherd too, and *you* are one of his sheep. Just as God cared about David, God cares about you too. You can be sure that God will lead you and guide you. And best of all, he will never, ever leave you, even in the scariest times. You never have to worry.

This is the same wonderful message that Jesus taught his followers one day on the hillsides of Lake Galilee …

Why Worry?

Matthew 6:25–34

One day, Jesus spoke to the people and said, "Don't worry. God wants you to be happy!"

Jesus pointed to the birds chirping around him. "The birds of the sky do not worry about where their next meal will come from. God takes care of them just as he will take care of you."

Jesus pointed to the flowers. "Look how God has clothed the flowers in the fields. Not even King Solomon looked as beautiful as these. God has provided for them, and he will also make sure you get what you need."

"Why don't you have more faith?" asked Jesus. "Do not worry about what you will eat, drink, or wear. Your heavenly Father knows you need these things. Instead," Jesus said, "spend your time and your energy working at following God's ways. Love God and follow his rules. Then God will provide for all your needs."

Jesus finished his sermon by saying, "So do not worry about tomorrow; it will have enough worries of its own. There is no need to add to the troubles each day brings."

THE
JESUS ANSWER

Wow! What a wonderful message from Jesus! Doesn't it make you feel special to know that God loves you so very much? Doesn't it make you smile to know that God cares about you more than anything else in the whole world? So now we know that the answer to our key question is "Yes! God cares about you!"

Believe!

❋

KEY IDEA:

I believe God is involved in and cares about my daily life.

KEY VERSE:

My help comes from the LORD. He is the Maker of heaven and earth.

—Psalm 121:2

CHAPTER 3

THINK

The Key Question:
How do I have a relationship with God?

Have you heard of the Garden of Eden? It was the very first garden God created—a beautiful, peaceful place where Adam and Eve lived. At first, everything was wonderful. God was the Father, and Adam and Eve were his children. They had a perfect relationship that should have lasted forever, but one day, something went wrong ...

Adam and Eve Disobey God
Genesis 2–3

God created the first man and woman on day six. Adam and Eve did everything together. And they spent time walking and talking with God. They were all very happy.

But Satan, God's enemy, could not stand God's perfect world. *I must do something!* Satan decided. So he made himself look like a snake and wrapped himself around the branch of the tree of wisdom. Satan stuck out his forked tongue to smell the ripe fruit from the beautiful tree.

"Simply scrumptious!" the snake hissed.

Eve heard the snake and asked, "What is scrumptious?"

The snake answered, "This fruit."

"That is the fruit from the tree of wisdom," said Eve. "God has said we can't eat from that tree. If we do, we will die."

"No! You won't die," said the snake. "God is afraid you will gain the knowledge of good and evil. If you eat the fruit you will be like God."

Eve wanted to eat some fruit, even though God had told her and Adam not to. So she took a bite. "Mmm," she said.

Adam saw that Eve didn't die when she ate the fruit. She offered him some, and Adam took a bite. Suddenly, Adam and Eve realized they were naked. They ran and hid in the bushes.

Then God called to Adam and Eve. They did not answer. But God knew where they were. "Why are you hiding from me?" he asked.

"We didn't want you to see us naked," Adam answered.

"You have eaten from the forbidden tree!" God said. "I love you both, but you may not live in my garden anymore."

It was a very sad day for everyone.

The Jump to Jesus

When Adam and Eve sinned, they had to leave the garden. They had to be separated from God. It looked like God's perfect relationship with his children was destroyed. But it wasn't.

God had a marvelous plan to put that relationship right again. He would show his people how their sins could be forgiven. God planned to send his only Son, Jesus, to die for our sins, to take all the blame on himself, so that we could be right with God again. And that is just what happened. Jesus died on the cross. And three days later, something amazing and wonderful and quite unbelievable happened …

He Has Risen!

Luke 24:1–12

Mary Magdalene, Joanna, and Mary, the mother of James, went to the tomb where Jesus' body had been taken after the crucifixion. When they arrived, they saw that the stone covering the opening of the tomb had been rolled away. They looked inside. Jesus was gone. "Where is our Lord?" they said.

Suddenly, two angels appeared. The women held each other in fear.

The angels said, "Why do you look for Jesus among the dead here in this tomb? He is not here. He has been raised from the dead! Don't you remember what he told you?"

The women shook their heads.

The angels' light shone like the sun. "Jesus told you the Son of Man would be handed over to sinners. They would crucify him, but death would not win. As foretold by the prophets, Jesus has now been raised up."

The women all agreed, "Yes! We do remember!"

Overjoyed at the good news, the three women ran back to where the disciples were staying. They burst into the room. "The Lord has risen!"

"You are beside yourselves with grief," said the disciples.

But Peter believed the women and ran to the tomb. There he saw Jesus' burial clothes lying on the floor. The tomb was empty. Peter returned to the disciples, amazed.

THE JESUS ANSWER

Jesus died, but he didn't stay dead. Death did not win. Life won; Jesus won; God won! When Jesus came back to life, God's marvelous plan worked. Sin could not separate us anymore from God, and God's relationship with his children was put right. Jesus died in our place, forgave our sins, and most wonderful of all, proved that there is eternal life—life that lasts forever, in heaven.

So how do you have a relationship with God? It's simple. God has done all the work. You just need to ask, to call to the Lord in prayer. You will be saved from sin and death, and have life everlasting with God.

Believe!

KEY IDEA:

I believe a person can have a relationship with God by God's grace through faith in Jesus Christ.

KEY VERSE:

God's grace has saved you because of your faith in Christ.

—Ephesians 2:8

CHAPTER 4

The Bible

THINK

The Key Question:
How do I know
God and his plan for my life?

In the Bible, God spoke to people all the time. God spoke to boys and girls, men and women. Sometimes he spoke out loud, and other times his message came through dreams. But whenever God spoke, his Word was powerful. And as people listened, they began to know God and understand his plan for their lives.

One man who listened to God was Moses, the leader of God's special people, the Israelites. God wanted to guide the Israelites, so he spoke to Moses and gave him ten rules for the Israelites to live by.

Old Testament

Rules to Live By

Exodus 20:1–17

Moses and the Israelites wandered in the desert. The people began doing whatever they liked. They didn't have any rules to live by. God told Moses to meet him on top of a mountain. There, God gave Moses a set of rules for his people to follow. These rules are called the Ten Commandments. After Moses left the mountain, he shared God's rules with the people.

Moses told them, "The most important rule is to love and worship God."

He also told them:

There is only one true God.
Do not worship other gods.
Never use God's name in a bad or angry way.
Always remember to keep one day each week special for God.
Treat your parents with respect.
Do not kill another human being.
Do not take another person's husband or wife for yourself.
Never take things that don't belong to you.
Do not say unkind things about other people.
It is not good to want what other people have.

Now Moses and his people knew how to live a life that would honor God and keep them from hurting themselves and other people.

The Jump to Jesus

Just like the Israelites used God's Word to guide them, Jesus used God's Word too. Jesus knew that every word that comes from God is powerful and true. And so when God's enemy, the devil, tried to trick Jesus, he knew that the words of Scripture—God's powerful Word, would help him win.

Jesus Is Tempted

Matthew 4:1–11

After Jesus was baptized, the Holy Spirit led him into the desert. Jesus didn't eat anything for forty days and forty nights. He was very hungry.

The devil came to Jesus and said, "If you are God's Son, order these stones to turn into bread."

Jesus said, "Human beings cannot live on bread alone, they need every word that God speaks."

Then the devil took Jesus to the top of the temple in the holy city of Jerusalem and said, "If you are God's Son, jump! For the Scripture says, 'God will command his angels to take care of you, and they will hold you up in their hands.'"

Jesus answered him, "But the Scripture also says, 'Do not put the Lord your God to the test.'"

Then the devil took Jesus to the top of a very high mountain and showed him the gold and jewels and power of all the kingdoms on earth. But there was one catch. The devil told Jesus he could have it all, but first, Jesus would have to kneel down and worship the devil.

"No!" Jesus said. "Go away, Satan! It is written, 'Worship the Lord your God, and serve him only!'"

Defeated, the devil finally left Jesus alone. Then angels came to take care of Jesus.

THE
JESUS ANSWER

So now we see how powerful and true God's Word in Scripture really is. If Jesus used God's Word to help and guide him, shouldn't we use it too? When we know God's Word, it can protect us, guide us, and help us. So if we really want to know God and his plan for our lives, we must read the Bible, listen to what God is saying, and believe!

Believe!

❈

KEY IDEA:

I believe the Bible is God's Word and it guides my beliefs and actions.

KEY VERSE:

God has breathed life into all Scripture. It is useful for teaching us what is true.

—2 Timothy 3:16

CHAPTER 5

Identity in Christ

THINK

The Key Question: Who am I?

Now if someone asked you the question, Who are you? you would tell them your name, wouldn't you? Names are important. Your name tells people who you are. Your name is special because your parents chose it just for you. But did you know that sometimes, in the Bible, God chose new names for his children? That is what happened one day to a man called Abram and his wife, Sarai.

God Changes Abram's and Sarai's Names

Genesis 12:1–8; 17:1–7, 15–17

Abram and Sarai lived in the country of Haran. They had everything they could ever want. They had a comfortable home, plenty of food on their table, and servants to help take care of their home and animals. But year after year, Sarai wanted and waited for a baby of her own.

One day, God came to Abram and said, "Leave your family and friends and go to a place I will show you. I will bless you with a large family, and you will always be remembered."

Abram didn't hesitate. Abram and Sarai believed God. They gathered all their things: their animals, their tents, and their servants. They asked their nephew Lot to come along with them. Then they said good-bye to everyone they knew. Together they set out for the unknown, knowing that the Lord had a great plan for them.

After they had traveled for some time, they came to the land of Canaan. The Lord appeared to Abram and said, "This is the land I will give your future family."

Abram was so happy that he built God an altar. Abram praised God because Canaan was so beautiful.

God was pleased with Abram. Abram had been faithful and trusting. So God decided to give Abram a new name. "Your name is no longer Abram. From now on you will be called Abraham, meaning the father of many nations. Sarai will now be called Sarah. She will be the mother of kings."

The Jump to Jesus

How wonderful for God to give Abraham and Sarah brand-new names. Now if God gave you a brand-new name, what name would you like him to choose? He might call you Precious, or Loved, or Chosen, or Special, or Treasured … because you are so much more than just a name to God. You are his own child and you belong to him.

When we realize that, we begin to understand just who we truly are. When we discover how much God treasures us, we can be changed in surprising ways too. This is what a man called Zacchaeus discovered one day. The day that Zacchaeus met Jesus, his name didn't change—but he *did!*

The Change in Zacchaeus

Luke 19:1–10

Zacchaeus was a rich man and the tax collector in the town of Jericho. Nobody liked him because he was greedy and took money that didn't belong to him. One day, Zacchaeus heard Jesus was coming to town. So he left his desk where he was counting money and went to find Jesus.

Many other people had come to see Jesus too. Crowds filled the streets, and Zacchaeus couldn't see over the heads of the taller people. Zacchaeus ran ahead of the crowd and climbed up into a tree. He watched as the crowd of people moved his way. Finally, he could see Jesus!

Jesus walked along the road and spoke to the crowd. When he looked up, he saw Zacchaeus sitting in the tree. Jesus called to him, "Come down and take me to your home."

"Me?" asked Zacchaeus. "You want to come to my house?" Zacchaeus scrambled down the tree. "I'm so happy! Come! We will have a feast."

The crowds grumbled and said, "Jesus is leaving us and going to a sinner's home."

Zacchaeus was amazed that Jesus wanted to spend time with him. "I am a changed man," Zacchaeus said to Jesus. "From now on, I'll give half of my possessions to the poor, and if I have cheated anyone out of anything, I will pay them back four times the amount."

Jesus was pleased and said, "I have come to find people who don't know God. I have come to save them. Today, *you* have been saved."

THE JESUS ANSWER

Do you know what happened to Zacchaeus after Jesus found him? He was like a brand-new person. God knew him. God loved him. And for the first time, Zacchaeus really knew who he was. He was not just a name. He was not just Zacchaeus. He was not just a tax collector. Zacchaeus knew he was a child of God; loved, special, and chosen; a one-of-a-kind, precious member belonging to God's big family. And that *is just who you are too!*

Believe!

KEY IDEA:

I believe I am significant because I am a child of God.

KEY VERSE:

Some people did accept him and did believe in his name. He gave them the right to become children of God.

— John 1:12

CHAPTER 6

Church

THINK

The Key Question:
How will God accomplish his plan?

From the very beginning of creation, God had a wonderful picture in his mind. In God's picture, the world he made was beautiful, and the togetherness he had with his people was perfect. It was a picture of one family with himself—the Father, Son, and Holy Spirit—at the center.

But when sin crept into the world, God's picture started to get spoiled. His people turned away from him. And so God started work on a marvelous plan to bring his people back to him. He chose an old man and an old woman to start a special family on earth. Through this community, God began to mend his relationship with his people. And it all happened one starry night …

Old Testament

God Builds a Nation

Genesis 15:1–7; 17:15–22; 18:10–15; 21:1–7

One evening, the sun sank from the sky, and the colors of orange and red faded to black. In the dark, God spoke to Abraham, "Look up to the heavens. Count the stars, if you can. I promise you will have as many children as there are stars in the sky."

Abraham believed the Lord.

The Lord said, "I will establish a covenant between us. I will be your God. And until the end of time, you and your children and your children's children will be my people. This land of Canaan, where you now live as an outsider, will be yours. I will give it to you and all the families after you. Forever and ever, I will be their God."

Even though Abraham believed God, years passed and Abraham and Sarah grew very, very old. They still did not have the family they yearned for.

One day, the Lord appeared to Abraham and said, "When I return to you next year, you and Sarah will have a son."

Sarah laughed when she heard the news. "How can an old woman have a baby?" she asked.

God asked Abraham, "Why does Sarah laugh? Is anything too hard for me to do?"

Sure enough, the Lord did as he promised. One year later, Abraham and Sarah had a beautiful baby boy. They named him Isaac.

Abraham raised his son and his household to love the Lord. He taught them what was right and just in the eyes of God. Eventually all the nations of the earth would be blessed because of Abraham's devotion to God.

The Jump to Jesus

Abraham's family grew and grew. Isaac's children had children and they had children who had more children. The family grew into a nation called Israel. Every day, God watched over the community of Israel as he worked to bring his people back to him. After many, many years, another baby was born. That baby's name was Jesus! He was the biggest blessing of all and the very best part of God's plan. Jesus came to make the relationship between God and his people better. But even though Jesus was everything the people hoped for, many of them did not believe in him.

Now, do you think God gave up on his plan? No! After Jesus rose from the dead and went back to heaven, God continued to build his relationship with his people through a new community called the church. The story of how the church was born is one of the most exciting stories you will ever read!

The Holy Spirit Comes to Establish the Church

Acts 2:1–41

After Jesus had risen, he knew that soon he would return to heaven. He told his disciples, "Stay together in the city. Don't leave until God sends you a special gift."

One morning, the disciples were together to celebrate the Feast of Pentecost. All of a sudden, a great rush of wind swirled around the room. Bright bursts of color that looked like flames appeared and settled on each person's head. The disciples fell to their knees praising God. Then they began to speak in many different languages.

Jewish people from all over the world were gathered together in Jerusalem. Each heard the disciples speaking to them in their own language. They wondered, "What does this mean? How do these local people speak languages from other places in the world?"

Peter, one of the disciples, stood up and shouted, "This means that God has sent us the gift of his Spirit. His Spirit lives in us so we can do unusual things. With the Spirit's power, we can speak in other languages. We can preach about God. We can perform miracles."

Peter explained, "God sent Jesus to earth as a man to serve the people. You heard Jesus teach. You saw his miracles. Then you put Jesus to death with the help of evil people. But that wasn't the end. God brought Jesus back to life. Death didn't stop Jesus. He came alive again. We have seen him alive. And we saw him return to heaven to be with God. Jesus promised not to forget us, so he sent the Holy Spirit to be with us. You can be sure of this—God made Jesus both Lord and Messiah."

The people were very upset by what Peter said. They remembered that Jesus told wonderful stories and did fantastic miracles. But they also remembered how they cheered when he died. Now they understood who Jesus really was—the Son of God! "What shall we do?" they cried.

"Change your ways, believe in Jesus, and be baptized," said Peter, "so that your sins may be forgiven. God's promise to send his Spirit is for you and your children and for everyone who believes in Jesus."

On that day, thousands of people accepted Jesus Christ as their Savior.

THE
JESUS ANSWER

What an exciting story! The day the Holy Spirit came was the day that God's church, his new family on earth, was born! After that day, the disciples traveled all over the world. They told everyone they met about God and invited people to join his church. God is still working on his plan to mend his relationship with his people. Every day, God uses the church to bring his people back to him. He will keep working, until the good news of Jesus has spread to every corner of the world. And some day Jesus will come back to earth. Then the beautiful picture in God's mind will be made new. It will be a wonderful picture of one family, with one faith, and one Father. And God's perfect relationship with his people will be mended.

Believe!

❈

KEY IDEA:
I believe God uses the church to bring about his plan.

KEY VERSE:
We will speak the truth in love. So we will grow up in every way to become the body of Christ.

— Ephesians 4:15

CHAPTER 7

Humanity

THINK

The Key Question: How does God see us?

When we ask the key question: *How does God see us?* what we really want to know is, *What does God think about us?* Or, *What does God see when he looks into our hearts?* And to answer that question, we have to go back to the very first people God created.

Do you remember the story of Adam and Eve, and how they had to leave the Garden of Eden because they disobeyed God? Let's find out what happened next …

Cain and Abel

Genesis 4:1–16

After leaving the Garden of Eden, Adam and Eve had two sons named Cain and Abel. Cain learned how to plant and harvest food. Abel learned how to be a shepherd.

Cain and Abel were good at their jobs. When the harvest was ripe, Cain gathered some of the grain and fruit he had grown and presented them to God. Abel presented his best firstborn lamb to God.

God was pleased with Abel. Abel gave God the best he had to give. But Cain took the best grain and fruit for himself and gave God what was left. God was disappointed with Cain. Cain became very unhappy and upset.

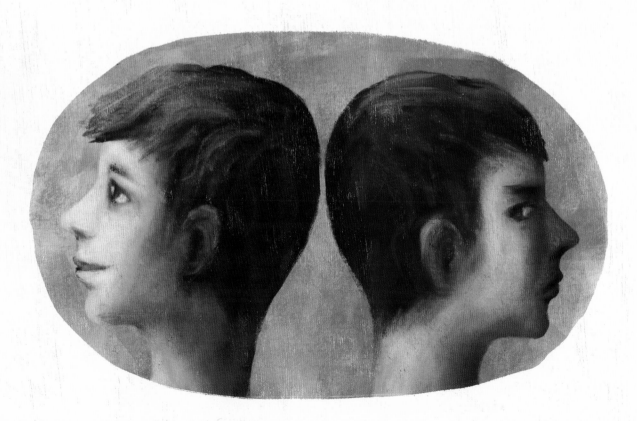

God asked Cain, "Why are you angry? You know that if you do what is right you will be accepted."

Cain didn't listen to God. He was jealous of Abel. And he was still very angry. So Cain invited Abel to go for a walk in his fields. While they were alone, Cain killed his brother.

God asked Cain, "Where's Abel?" Cain didn't answer. But the Lord God knew what Cain had done. He knew Cain had sinned.

God said, "You can't stay here. You can't be a farmer anymore. You'll spend the rest of your life wandering, looking for a place to live."

So Cain left his family and traveled to another land.

The Jump to Jesus

How sad it must have been for God to see all that anger, jealousy, and fighting in the people he made. Sin was like a disease that spread through Adam and Eve, and then Cain, and then through the whole world. But do you know something amazing? God still loved Cain and protected him. Even though God could see all that sin when he looked into Cain's heart, he saw something else too. God saw his own child, his own wonderful creation. He saw someone he made to be just like God himself, someone he delighted in. And so God never gave up on Cain, and he never gave up on the world. God kept looking for ways to save his people from their sin.

How could he rescue his people? How could he get them back on the right path when they wandered away, like little lost sheep? There was only one way. God needed a shepherd—a "super shepherd" who would do anything to save his sheep. And Jesus, the best and bravest super shepherd the world had ever known, would come to rescue us all, just like the shepherd in this story …

The Lost Sheep Is Found

Matthew 18:10–14

Thousands of people came to hear Jesus tell them about God and his Kingdom. Jesus often told the people stories that would help them understand his teachings. The people who gathered around Jesus were ordinary people—farmers and shepherds, mothers and merchants, and their children. So Jesus used everyday events when he told his stories. One day, he told them this story of the good shepherd:

There once was a shepherd who had one hundred sheep. One day, a sheep wandered away from the rest of the flock. The shepherd knew the sheep was in danger because bears and lions lived in the hills. He was very worried. He didn't want to lose even one of his sheep. What should he do?

The shepherd decided to leave the other ninety-nine and look for his one little lost sheep. He searched and searched. He searched up one hill and down another. He looked behind huge rocks and bushes and down in the gullies.

Finally, the shepherd found his sheep. He was so happy!

"Hurray!" he said to his sheep. "You were lost and now you are found!" Instead of scolding it, the shepherd led his wandering sheep back to the flock.

Jesus told this story to show us that God the Father is like the shepherd. He loves each and every one of us. We are all special to him. He does not want to lose even one of us.

God never wants us to run away from him, but if we do, he will come looking for us.

THE
JESUS ANSWER

How wonderful to know that God never gives up on us. Even when we wander away and do things wrong. God sees us as his precious child. Someone he keeps searching for with a love that is so much stronger than all our sin. God's love and forgiveness is for all who will come to him, for anyone and everyone who believes in Jesus. Now if we could love each other the way God loves us, imagine what a wonderful world that would be.

Believe!

❋

KEY IDEA:
I believe all people are loved by God and need Jesus Christ as their Savior.

KEY VERSE:
God so loved the world that he gave his one and only Son.
Anyone who believes in him will not die but will have eternal life.

— John 3:16

Compassion

THINK

The Key Question:
What should we do about people in need?

Ever since the beginning of time, people all over the world have asked the question, What should we do about people in need? They wonder, How can we help people who are not treated the right way, or those who cannot take care of themselves?

God gives us the answer in the Bible. He is full of love and concern for everyone because he made all human beings. And he wants his followers to be part of the answer. He wants us to take care of the poor. He wants us to help those who are in need. And in the Bible, we find a beautiful story about people who did just that …

Ruth and Boaz
Ruth 1–4

Naomi and Ruth were very sad. Their husbands had died, and all through the land of Moab people were hungry. Naomi didn't want to stay in a foreign land any longer. She decided to return to her family in the town of Bethlehem where there was food.

Ruth, Naomi's daughter-in law, begged to go with Naomi. But Naomi told Ruth to stay with her people in the land of Moab. Naomi cared for Ruth and wanted her to get married again and have a family.

But Ruth told her, "Where you go I will go. Where you stay I will stay. Your people will be my people. Your God will be my God." So Ruth followed Naomi to Bethlehem.

Naomi and Ruth didn't have husbands to take care of them and find them food. They had to take care of themselves. Naomi's cousin Boaz had a farm, so Ruth said to Naomi, "Let me go into the fields. I will pick up the leftover grain from the harvest."

Ruth worked hard gathering grain out of Boaz's fields. When Boaz returned to his field, he saw Ruth searching for the leftover grain. Boaz was kind and welcomed Ruth to take as much grain as she needed from his fields.

"Why are you so kind to me?" Ruth asked Boaz.

"I heard how devoted you are to Naomi," he said.

That day, Ruth returned to Naomi with plenty of food. Naomi was grateful to Boaz for being kind and compassionate to Ruth.

Naomi wanted Ruth to be happy and to marry again. She told Ruth to go back to Boaz. Ruth listened and went to him. Boaz saw she was kind and good. He gave her more food to take home to Naomi. Then Boaz went to the town's men and asked them to let him marry Ruth. They agreed. So Ruth and Boaz were married.

Soon Ruth had a baby boy. Both Ruth and Naomi praised God who had given them a new family.

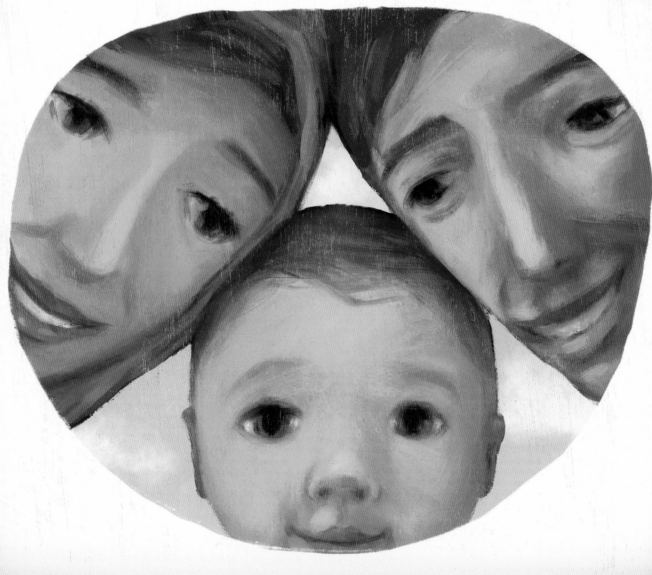

The Jump to Jesus

Don't you think that God must have smiled when he saw how kind Ruth was to Naomi? Don't you think he was pleased when Boaz took care of them both? The story of how Boaz cared for Ruth and Naomi is a beautiful picture of how God cares for us.

When Jesus came to earth, he gave us another picture of how we are to help take care of those in need. One day, he told a story about a man who was robbed and the good neighbor who came to help him.

The Good Samaritan

Luke 10:25–37

A lawyer and Jesus were talking one day. The lawyer wanted to test Jesus. He said, "What must I do to be saved?"

Jesus asked, "What do you think the law says?"

The lawyer responded, "You should love God completely, and you should love your neighbor as you love yourself."

The lawyer then asked, "Lord, who is my neighbor?"

To answer, Jesus told this story:

A man was walking down the road. Robbers jumped out of the bushes and attacked the man. They beat him and stole everything, even his clothes. Then they ran away and left the man in the road, dying.

A temple priest came walking down the same road. He saw the man but kept walking as if the injured man were not there. Another man who worked in the temple came along. He, too, saw the man lying in the road bleeding. He crossed the road and walked by on the other side.

Later a third man came along. He was a Samaritan traveler. He saw the man who had been left to die. He stopped. He cradled the victim's head in his lap as he gave him a drink. He carefully wrapped his body in a blanket and gently laid the man on his donkey. He took him to an inn.

The Samaritan told the innkeeper, "Take care of this man until I return. Here is enough money to cover all the expenses. I will come back soon. If his care costs more than I left you, I will pay you then."

Jesus asked the lawyer, "Who was the good neighbor in the story?"

The lawyer answered, "The one who cared for the injured man."

Jesus said, "Go and be a good neighbor."

THE
JESUS ANSWER

Can you see how that story helps to answer our key question about the poor and those who are not treated well? That good, kind neighbor was the answer. And you can be part of the answer too. When you find ways to take care of others, or help the poor, or show kindness to someone in need, you are not just being a good neighbor. You are not just being like Ruth and Boaz or the good Samaritan. You are being like Jesus. And that is just what God wants.

Believe!

❊

KEY IDEA:
I believe God calls all Christians to show compassion to people in need.

KEY VERSE:
Save those who are weak and needy.

— Psalm 82:4

CHAPTER 9

Stewardship

THINK

The Key Question:
What is God's call on my life?

This wonderful world in which we live belongs to God. He created it. He is the owner. Our job is to take good care of it. But did you know that it's not just the earth that belongs to God? In the Bible, Psalm 24 has a beautiful verse that says, The earth belongs to the LORD. And so does everything in it. The world belongs to him. And so do all those who live in it. Wow! Does that mean that you belong to God? Yes, you do! Does that mean that everything you have, and everything you own, really belongs to God? Yes, it's true!

Before we find the answer to the question, What is God's call on my life? we have to begin to understand that our lives are not really our own at all—our lives belong to God. And Hannah and Samuel's story teaches us just that …

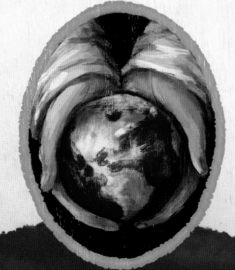

Old Testament

Hannah and Samuel
1 Samuel 1:1–28; 3:1–11

Hannah loved God. But she was sad, for she had no children. Each year, her husband took her to a place called Shiloh, and Hannah prayed a special prayer that God would give her a child. One year, she prayed, "Dear God, if you will only give me a son, I will give him back to you, to serve you all his days." She prayed so hard her mouth moved, but no words came out. A priest asked if she was drunk. "No," she said. "I'm pouring my heart out to God."

"May you find favor in God's eyes," said the priest.

The following year, Hannah's prayers were answered. She had a new baby boy named Samuel! She happily cared for Samuel until he was old enough to leave her. Then she kept her promise to God and took Samuel to live with the priests in Shiloh.

God gave Hannah many more children. And Hannah was pleased to know that Samuel was growing up in Shiloh, where he would love and serve God always.

One night in the temple, Samuel heard someone call his name. He sat up and rubbed his eyes. He thought Eli the priest had called him, so he ran to Eli.

"Here I am," Samuel said.

Eli said, "I did not call you. Go back to bed."

A while later Samuel heard his name being called again. He ran to Eli and said, "Here I am."

Eli shook his head. "I did not call you. Go back to sleep."

A third time, Samuel heard his name called! He ran to Eli again. "Here I am."

Eli finally understood. He said, "God is calling you, Samuel. Go to sleep. When you hear your name called again, answer, 'Your servant is listening.'"

That's exactly what Samuel did. God called Samuel again that night and Samuel listened. Samuel shared what God said to him with the people. And Samuel did God's work the rest of his life.

The Jump to Jesus

It must have been so hard for Hannah to give Samuel back to God. But Hannah knew something special. Hannah knew that Samuel did not really belong to her. Samuel belonged to God. When Hannah gave Samuel back, she was really just giving back what already belonged to God. And how wonderful for little Samuel to be called by God!

Now if you belong to God, he calls out to you too. God calls us, no matter how young or old we are, to find ways to give back to him. And one day, Jesus saw a woman who did that very thing …

New Testament

A Widow's Gift
Mark 12:38–44

One day, Jesus was teaching his people. As he spoke, Jesus warned his disciples, "Watch out for the teachers of the law. They dress in fancy clothes. They expect people to treat them better than anyone else. They take the best seats in the synagogues for themselves. They show off, praying long prayers, and yet they treat poor widows badly. The day is coming when these men will be severely punished for their actions."

Jesus said, "I am going to tell you the truth. The rich people give a portion of their wealth to the church. They come to the synagogue and meet and greet each other. Then they place their gifts in the synagogue's treasury. At the end of the day, they go home to fine houses and plenty of food on their tables. They continue to dress in their fine clothes and eat the best food. The rich do not feel the loss of the money they gave the treasury. It was just the extra money they had.

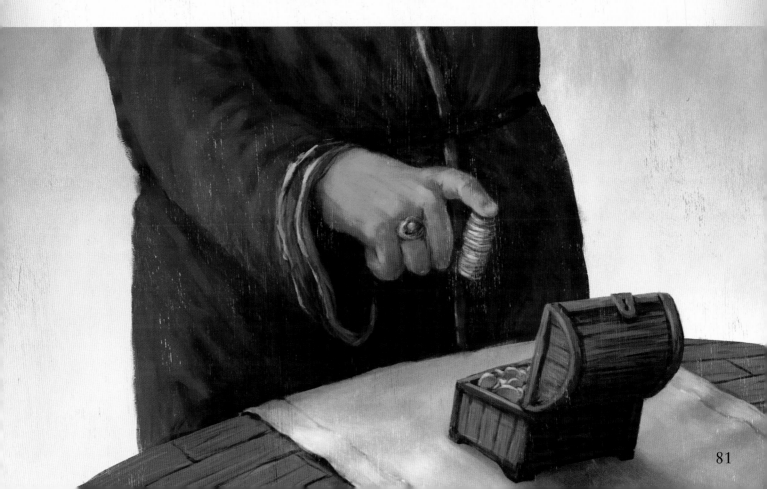

"Now look over there. Do you see that poor widow? She came to the temple and dropped two small coins into the treasury. Two small coins don't seem like much, but that was all she had to live on. She doesn't know where her next meal will come from. But she put God first and gave him everything she had. Her gift appears small, but it is more generous than the money given by the rich. The widow's gift truly is the most generous gift of all."

THE
JESUS ANSWER

Can you see how the poor widow gave everything she had back to God? She knew that her money belonged to him. And when we realize that everything we have—our money, our bodies, our homes, and our lives— belong to God, then we can try to give back to him too. So how can we do that? We can be generous with our money. We can take good care of our bodies. We can invite friends into our homes and share our food and toys with them. We can pray and ask God to show us how to live our lives for him. These are all wonderful ways to give back to God— because everything belongs to him. And when we do that, we will truly be answering God's call on our life.

Believe!

✽

KEY IDEA:
I believe everything I am and everything I own belong to God.

KEY VERSE:
The earth belongs to the LORD. And so does everything in it.

—Psalm 24:1

CHAPTER 10

Eternity

THINK

The Key Question: What happens next?

Have you ever read a story that was so exciting you couldn't wait to find out the end? Or maybe you've watched a wonderful movie that you liked a lot because it had a really happy ending. Happy endings are wonderful. And you know what? When we believe in Jesus, our lives will have a very happy ending. We don't have to worry about what happens next.

The Bible says that when we reach the end of this life here on earth, there's a brand-new life waiting for us in heaven! It will be like turning the page and finding the most exciting and wonderful ending we could ever imagine. Let's find out what happened one day to Elijah and Elisha as they walked together—these two friends couldn't believe what happened next!

Elijah Goes to Heaven
2 Kings 2:1–17

The prophet Elijah was a godly man. He told people about the one true God. He tried to teach kings about God, and he didn't stop, even though they became angry. Some people who didn't believe in God tried to have Elijah killed. But Elijah never stopped loving God.

After many years, the Lord was ready to take Elijah away to be with him in heaven. Three times, the Lord God told Elijah to go to special places. Faithful Elijah listened and went where God told him: first to Bethel, then to Jericho, and finally to the Jordan River. Each time Elijah told his follower, Elisha, to stay behind. But Elisha said, "As surely as the Lord lives and as you live, I will not leave you."

Elijah and Elisha stood at the bank of the Jordan River. Fifty of God's prophets watched them from a distance. Elijah took off the cloak he was wearing. He rolled it up and struck the water with his cloak. The water divided, making a dry path. Then Elijah and Elisha walked through the river.

When they were on the other side of the Jordan River, Elijah asked Elisha, "What can I do for you before I am taken from you?"

"Let me carry on your ministry," Elisha replied.

"That is a difficult request," Elijah answered. "But if you see me taken away, then you will receive it."

Suddenly a fiery chariot attached to horses of fire appeared out of heaven. It swooped down and scooped up Elijah, taking him to heaven. Elisha saw Elijah taken away to be with the Lord God. He watched in amazement as the burning chariot and horses carried Elijah away and disappeared through the clouds. "My father! My father!" he cried out. "The chariots and horsemen of Israel!" And that was the last time Elisha saw his friend.

Then the Spirit of God rested on Elisha and he took over Elijah's ministry. The fifty prophets saw this happen and were witnesses to God's power in Elisha. From then on, Elisha followed Elijah's ways and honored God.

The Jump to Jesus

Wow! What an amazing sight it must have been to see Elijah being carried off to heaven in a chariot of fire. But don't you wonder what heaven looks like? Don't you wonder what it will be like when we get there?

Jesus talked a lot about heaven. He said that heaven is a wonderful home, with room for everyone. Jesus told us that he would get heaven ready for us, and that he would be waiting when we arrived. How exciting! In the very last book of the Bible, there is a beautiful story that describes what heaven will be like.

John's Vision of Heaven
Revelation 4:1–8; 7:9; 21:11–22

John was a disciple of Jesus who told others everything Jesus had done on earth. But the people in charge didn't like what John had to say. They punished him and sent him away to an island called Patmos. While John was all alone, Jesus sent an angel to comfort him. Jesus wanted John to tell all Christians, "Don't be discouraged. Don't give up, even when you are being punished for believing in Jesus. You will see your reward in heaven for your faithfulness."

Then John had visions of heaven. He saw what it will be like when Jesus takes his believers home to heaven.

In John's vision, people from all over the earth were gathered around God's throne. They sang praises to God together and worshipped him. The one who sat on the throne glistened like sparkling jewels. A rainbow as green as an emerald circled around the throne. And everyone sang together: "Holy, holy, holy is the Lord God Almighty, who was, and is, and is to come."

Someday there will be a new heaven and a new earth. All sadness, crying, sickness, and death will be gone. The new city of God will be enormous and beautiful. A spectacular wall will surround the city like a glittering rainbow made of millions of colorful jewels. And there will be twelve giant gates in the wall, each made of solid pearl. The gates of the city will always be open to welcome God's people any time of the day or night. The streets will be polished with gold that glistens like glass.

At the end, there will be no need for a temple, for the Father and Son will be there. There will be no need for the sun or the moon, for God's glory will be brighter than the summer sun.

A crystal-clear river of life will flow from the throne of God and through the city. The tree of life will grow there. New fruit will grow on its branches. And the leaves of this tree will heal all the nations.

Jesus said, "Behold, I am coming soon! I am the First and the Last, the Beginning and the End. Yes, I am coming soon."

Amen. Come, Lord Jesus.

THE
JESUS ANSWER

Now close your eyes. Can you see that wonderful picture of heaven in your mind? Can you see the big, beautiful gates that are always open? Can you see the streets of gold and the colorful jewels sparkling everywhere? Can you hear the sounds of laughter and angels singing? Can you see Jesus with his arms stretched out wide to welcome you? Heaven is what happens next. Heaven is our wonderful happy ending. When we finish our lives here on earth, it will be our new home ... where we will live with God forever.

Believe!

✻

KEY IDEA:

I believe there is a heaven and a hell and that Jesus will return to establish his eternal kingdom.

KEY VERSE:

Do not let your hearts be troubled ... There are many rooms in my Father's house.

—John 14:1–2

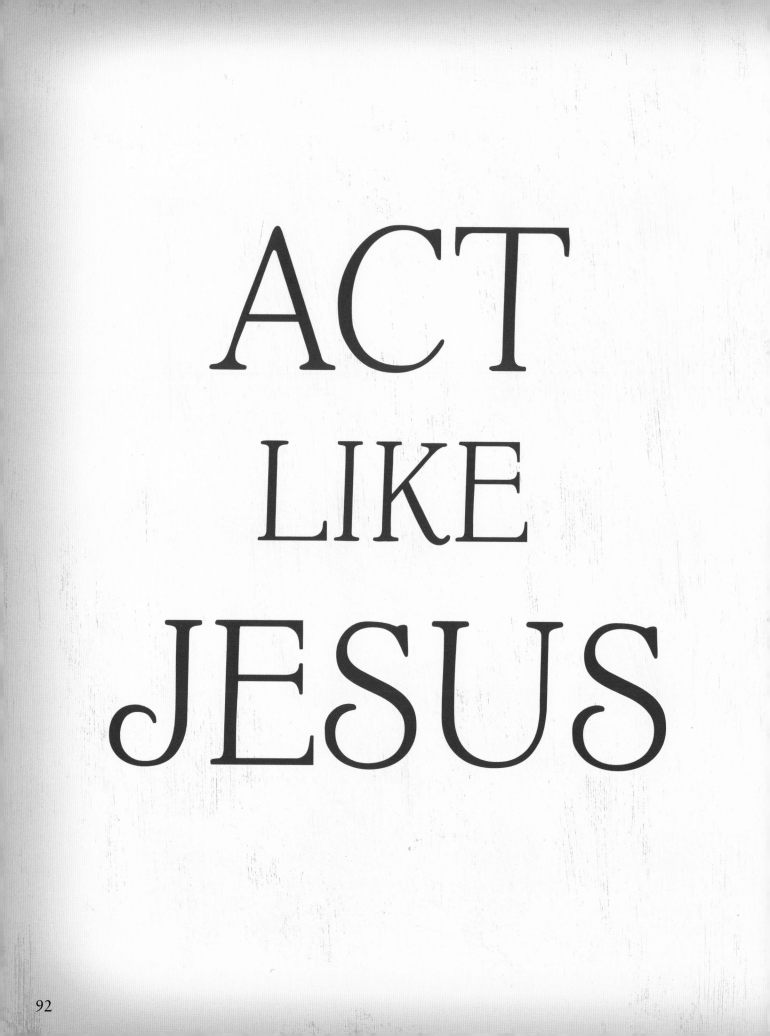

ACT
LIKE
JESUS

CHAPTER 11

Worship

ACT

The Key Question:
How do I honor God
in the way he deserves?

One of the very best ways for us to honor God is to worship him. Worship means praising God for who he is and what he has done for us. In Bible times, people praised God in many different places. They praised him on towering mountaintops, inside homes with dirt floors, in beautiful churches, and even inside dark prisons. And people worshiped God in many different ways. They sang or danced; they gave gifts to God or prayed. But what is most important to God is not *where* we worship him or *how* we worship him. What really matters to God is that our worship comes from the heart.

God wants us to love and worship him above everything else, and Daniel was someone who did just that. Let's find out what happened to Daniel when he was taken away to Babylon …

Daniel Only Worships God
Daniel 6

God's prophets told the Israelites not to forget about God. But the Israelites ignored them. Their lives did not please God. Finally, the powerful Babylonians conquered the Israelites. Daniel, along with many of God's people, was taken as a slave to Babylon.

Daniel became a trustworthy, hardworking, godly man. He was a great prophet of God. Daniel was also the favorite servant of King Darius. This made all the king's other servants jealous. They wanted to get rid of Daniel.

The king's servants knew Daniel prayed to God every day. They said, "We will get the king to make a law against praying to God."

"King Darius, you alone are the almighty!" they said. "Make a law against worshiping anyone besides you. Then whoever breaks the law will be thrown to the lions!"

King Darius signed the new law. The king's servants waited and watched for Daniel to pray.

"King Darius!" the wicked servants said, "Daniel has broken your law! We saw him praying to his God."

King Darius was very sad. He loved Daniel. He tried to stick up for Daniel. But the mean servants said, "King Darius, you made the law unbreakable!" So King Darius had no choice. The king's soldiers grabbed Daniel, took him to the lions' den, and threw him in.

"May the God you love save you," King Darius told Daniel. Then the king returned home, deeply sad. He worried all night.

Early the next morning, the king rushed to the lions' den. He called, "Daniel! Has your God protected you?"

Daniel answered, "I am safe! My God sent his angel to close the lions' mouths."

King Darius rejoiced. He told the whole kingdom, "Daniel's God is the living God. He is a deliverer and a Savior!"

The Jump to Jesus

Can you see how Daniel put God first? It would have been so easy for him to worship King Darius, but Daniel would only worship God. Imagine how Daniel must have sung praises to God after he had saved him from the lions! Daniel truly worshiped God from his heart.

But did you know that when Jesus came to earth he saw some people who just *pretended* to worship God? Jesus saw people who *said* they loved God. They talked about God a lot. They said their prayers really loud so that everyone could hear. They *looked* like they were worshiping God. But Jesus could see into their hearts. Jesus knew they were not honoring God in the way he deserved. Jesus reminded them that the only way to truly honor God is to love him with all your heart, soul, mind, and strength. In the next story we will hear about two men who worshiped God just like that. But they were not in a church—they were in (of all places) a prison cell!

Paul and Silas Worship God in Prison

Acts 16:16–35

Paul and Silas traveled to the city of Ephesus to tell people about Jesus. But not everyone in the city wanted to hear about him. Some people were mad and complained to the city officials. They decided to attack Paul and Silas to make them leave. Paul and Silas were badly beaten and thrown into jail. The jailer put them in the inner cell and locked them in chains so they could not escape.

During the night, Paul and Silas prayed and sang songs to God. The other prisoners listened. Suddenly a violent earthquake shook the prison. All the prison doors opened, and everyone's chains broke off.

The jailer woke up and thought the prisoners had escaped. He was so afraid he wanted to kill himself. But Paul shouted, "Stop! Don't kill yourself! We are all here."

The jailer fell down in front of Paul and Silas. He asked, "What must I do to be saved?"

They replied, "Believe in the Lord Jesus." Then they told everyone about Jesus.

The jailer washed their cuts and bandaged them. He brought Paul and Silas to his house and fed them. Paul and Silas told the jailer, his family, and his servants about Jesus. Then they baptized everyone in the jailer's house. The jailer was full of joy because he, his family, and his servants were saved.

THE
JESUS ANSWER

Now do you think Paul and Silas were pretending to worship God when they were in that prison cell? No! They were truly worshiping God from the heart. And how wonderful that after God saved them, the jailer's whole family began to worship God too. So how can *we* truly worship God from the heart?

One of the best ways is to gather together with *our* church family. When we take time to sing praise to God for who he is and what he has done for us, when we pray and read the Bible, when we share communion together, we are remembering Jesus, loving God with all we have, and honoring him in the way he deserves.

Believe!

❉

KEY IDEA:

I worship God for who he is and what he has done for me.

KEY VERSE:

Come, let us sing for joy to the LORD. Let us give a loud shout to the Rock who saves us.

—*Psalm 95:1*

CHAPTER 12

Prayer

ACT

The Key Question:
How do I grow by communicating with God?

Imagine you have a very good friend—a friend you talk with every day. What would you talk about? You would talk together about what is happening every day in your life. You might tell your friend if you were feeling unhappy or afraid, and they would listen and try to help you. As you and your friend talk together, you grow closer to each other. Did you know that God is like a very good friend too? God wants you to talk to him every day, just like you would talk to your friend.

When we talk to God it is called prayer. And prayer is one of the best ways to communicate with God. The Bible is full of stories about people who talked with God, especially when they needed his help. One of those people was a man named Gideon.

Gideon Talks to God

Judges 6–7

Long after God's people settled in the Promised Land, the Israelites forgot to obey God again. They hid in the hills, afraid of their enemy, the Midianites. One day, a man named Gideon heard an angel say, "God is with you, mighty warrior!"

"God is with me?" asked Gideon. "Then why are we having such troubles?"

"You will save Israel," said the angel. "God has chosen you to lead your people."

"Me?" cried Gideon. "But who will listen to me? I am no one!"

"God will go with you," said the angel.

But Gideon wasn't so sure. So he said to God, "You promised to help me save Israel. If that's true, give me a sign. I'll put a piece of wool on the ground. If tomorrow morning the wool is wet from the dew, but the ground is dry, I'll know you'll help me."

That's exactly what happened. The next morning, Gideon checked the piece of wool. It was soaking wet with dew, but the ground was dry. Gideon still wasn't sure. So he talked to God again.

"Don't be angry with me, God. But can I ask you for another sign? This time make the ground wet and the fleece dry." That night, God did just that. The next morning, the fleece was dry, but the ground was soaking wet from heavy dew.

So Gideon made plans to fight the Midianites. Thousands of men came together to help him. But God said to Gideon, "That's too many men. Send back any who are afraid." So Gideon let 22,000 men leave. Now, 10,000 were left.

"You still have too many," said God. He showed Gideon who to send home. Now only 300 men were left. God told Gideon's army to surround the Midianite camp. When Gideon gave the signal, they surrounded the camp. They smashed jars, waved torches, yelled loudly, and blew their trumpets. The Midianites didn't know what was happening. They grabbed their swords and fought against themselves. Then they ran away. God used Gideon's tiny army to win the battle.

The Jump to Jesus

Did you see how Gideon listened to God and how God helped and guided him? Jesus knew God would help and guide him too, and he talked to God all the time. Even though Jesus was so busy, he always found time to be alone with God, to pray, and to listen to what his Father told him. And one day, Jesus taught his disciples how to pray . . .

Jesus Teaches His Disciples to Pray
Luke 11:1–13

One day, Jesus was praying. When he finished, one of his disciples asked him, "Lord teach us how to pray."

So Jesus told them to pray like this:

"'Father,
may your name be honored.
May your kingdom come.
Give us each day our daily bread.
Forgive us our sins,
as we also forgive everyone
who sins against us.
Keep us from falling into sin
when we are tempted.'"

The disciples learned this prayer and passed it on to other people who believed in Jesus. Then Jesus told his disciples a story. "A man went to his friend's house in the middle of the night. He asked his friend for some bread because he didn't have anything to feed his guest. But the friend told the man to go away because they were sleeping. The man didn't leave. He kept knocking on the door until the friend opened it and gave him the bread he wanted."

Jesus ended the story and said, "The friend did not get out of bed because of their friendship. The friend got up because the man was so bold and kept knocking. He gave the man the bread he wanted."

Then Jesus told them, "If you ask, it will be given to you. If you look, you will find. If you knock, the door will open for you. God will give to anyone who asks in his name."

THE
JESUS ANSWER

Did you recognize the prayer that Jesus taught his disciples? It's the same prayer you may have heard in church, or maybe you say it with your family at home. What Jesus taught his disciples on that day long ago is the same lesson he teaches us now. Talk to God. Tell him everything. Ask him anything. Never give up. God is always listening. And as you pray, you will grow closer to God. He will help you. You will feel his peace in your heart.

Believe!

❃

KEY IDEA:

I pray to God to know him and find direction in my life.

KEY VERSE:

God has surely listened. He has heard my prayer ... He has not held back his love from me.

—*Psalm 66:19-20*

CHAPTER 13

Bible Study

ACT

The Key Question: How do I study God's Word?

Suppose you are traveling somewhere new with your family. You pack your bags, climb in the car, and fasten your seatbelts. But how do you know which way to go? You would probably check a map—maybe one in a book or one that shows up on a little screen in your car. As you follow that map, it guides you all the way to where you are going.

Our lives are a bit like taking a journey. We need a road map too, to show us which way to go. But our road map is the Bible, God's Word. When we read God's Word and listen to what it says, God guides us and shows us the right way to go in life. God reminded Joshua to do this one day before he started on a very special journey ...

God Tells Joshua to Remember the Law

Joshua 1:1–11

God's people were ready to enter the land that God had promised them. Moses, their first leader had died, so God appointed Joshua to be their new leader. The Lord spoke to Joshua, "My friend Moses is dead. Now I'm giving you a big job. You're going to lead the Israelites to the land I promised to give them. Tell everyone to get ready. You're going to take them across the Jordan River. I'm going to give them all the land they walk on because I promised Moses I would.

"Your land will stretch from the desert to Lebanon, and from the great river Euphrates all the way to the Mediterranean Sea in the west. No one will be able to fight you and win. I stood by Moses. Now I'll stand by you. I'll never leave you or give up on you. Joshua, be strong, brave, and courageous. The Israelites need you.

"You must obey the laws I gave Moses. If you follow all the laws, you will be successful. Never stop talking about the Book of the Law. Think about the laws day and night. That way you will never forget my words on how to live. Do not be afraid. Do not lose hope. I am the Lord your God. I will be with you wherever you go."

Joshua told his officers to spread the news. They told the Israelites to get their things together. Everyone was happy. They were going to cross the Jordan River and finally live in the land God promised.

The Jump to Jesus

Do you want to know what happened next in the story of Joshua? He did cross the Jordan River. Joshua did lead God's people into the Promised Land. He used God's Word to help him get there, just like a road map. Joshua remembered all the words that God had spoken to him. He never forgot the laws God had given Moses. God's Word guided Joshua all through his life. And God's Word can guide us all through our lives too.

So where do we find God's Word? It is written for us in the Bible. When we pick up our Bibles and turn the pages, we are reading God's own words to us. We can hear what God has to say. But there's more to it than just hearing God's Word. When Jesus came, he told a special story about four different kinds of people who all heard God's Word. As you read this story, try to decide which kind of person you would want to be.

Jesus Teaches about Four Kinds of Soil
Matthew 13:1–23

Jesus liked to teach the people by telling stories. One day, Jesus spoke to a large crowd standing on the shore of the lake. He said, "A farmer went out to sow his seeds. As he scattered the seeds, they fell all over the place. Some seeds fell on the path, and the birds ate the seeds. Other seeds fell on rocky ground with a little soil. Those seeds sprang up quickly in the shallow dirt. Then the sun grew hot. The plants got burnt and died. Other seeds fell among thorny plants. The thorns grew up and choked the good plants. Still other seeds fell on good soil. The seeds that fell on the good soil started to grow right away. They grew and grew and filled the whole field."

Then Jesus explained what the story meant. "The seed story is about different kinds of people who hear the word of God. The seeds that fall on the path are like people who hear about God and don't understand. Their hearts never get to know God. The seeds that fall on rocky ground are like people who hear the word of God with joy. But because they don't keep learning about God, they give up when things get tough. The seeds that fall in the thorns are like people who hear about God, but they let worry, lies, and greed take over their faith.

"But the seed falling on good soil is like the person who hears the word and understands it. This person believes in God and shares their faith with other people. And more and more people come to love God."

THE
JESUS ANSWER

Now which person in that story would you want to be like? Wouldn't you want to be like the last person, the one who helped the seeds of God's love grow? Jesus doesn't want us to just hear *God's Word. Jesus wants us to really study those words. So how do we do that? We read our Bible and pray, we learn about God and his truth, we believe, and then we act on it. If you can do that, you will help God's seeds of love grow and grow. And the Bible will become your road map, guiding you along your journey through life. It's like a bright light shining down on the path, showing you the way to go.*

Believe!

✿

KEY IDEA:
I study the Bible to know God and his truth and to find direction for my daily life.

KEY VERSE:
The word of God is alive and active.

—*Hebrews 4:12*

Single-Mindedness

ACT

The Key Question:
How do I keep my focus on Jesus?

Have you ever been so busy playing with your toys that you didn't know your mom was there? Or maybe one day you were having so much fun playing with your friends that you didn't hear your mom calling you? When that happens, what does your mom do? She may say something like "look at me" because she wants you to turn your eyes toward her. Your mom doesn't want to be ignored or forgotten.

Did you know God feels the same way? God wants us to know he is there. God wants us to put him first, above everything else. God wants us to listen to him and obey, so that he can guide us in our life. No matter how busy we are, no matter what is going on, he wants us to stay focused on him. King Jehoshaphat was someone who knew how to do just that ...

Jehoshaphat Prays to God for Help
2 Chronicles 20:1–30

The kingdom of Judah was small compared to the big nations around it. But this kingdom was God's kingdom and these were God's people. One day, some men came to the palace and warned King Jehoshaphat, "A big enemy army is moving this way. They are coming to fight us!"

Jehoshaphat was worried, but he prayed to God. Then Jehoshaphat ordered the people not to eat anything and focus their attention on praying. He told them to pray for God to help them.

Jehoshaphat went to the temple of the Lord and prayed.

"Lord, God of our people, you rule over all nations. You're strong and no one can beat you. Lord, you gave this land to your people forever. They live here. They built a place of worship for your Name. We know that when we cry out to you, you will hear us."

As they went out to face the enemy army, Jehoshaphat said, "Listen. Have faith in the Lord your God. God will take care of you. Have faith and you will be successful." Then a large group of men marched in front of God's army and sang:

"Give thanks to the Lord, for his love endures forever."

While they sang their praises to God, the Lord saved Jehoshaphat and his people. He made the enemy army fight each other. Soon the enemy was no longer a threat to God's people.

All the men of Judah returned safe and happy to Jerusalem. They sang songs and played instruments thanking God. And the kingdom of Jehoshaphat was at peace.

The Jump to Jesus

Wow! God saved King Jehoshaphat and all his people. Did you notice how Jehoshaphat kept his eyes on God, even though he could have been distracted and worried about that big army? Jehoshaphat knew how important it was to keep his focus on God by praying and trusting God to help him.

Jesus knew how important it was to keep his focus on God too. Jesus always put God first. The Bible says that Jesus often went up into the hills to pray to God and to be alone with his Father. The next story begins right on one of those hills …

Jesus Walks on Water

Matthew 14:22–33

Jesus needed time with his Father. So he went into the hills to pray.

As the sun set, the disciples got into a boat to sail across the lake. But when it became dark, the wind began to stir the waves, tossing the small boat back and forth. Then in the middle of the night, the disciples noticed something strange. A man walked toward them right on top of the water.

"It's a ghost!" they cried in terror.

"Don't be afraid!" called Jesus. "It is I."

Peter yelled, "If it's you, Lord, tell me to come to you!" Jesus called, and Peter climbed out of the boat. He too began to walk on the water. But when his eyes looked away from Jesus and down at the stormy sea, Peter began to sink. "Help me, Lord!" he cried. Jesus grabbed Peter's hand and pulled him out of the waves.

"Peter, where's your faith?" asked Jesus as they climbed into the boat.

But Peter and the other disciples could only bow down before Jesus. "You really are the Son of God!" they said.

THE
JESUS ANSWER

Did you notice what happened to Peter as soon as he took his eyes off Jesus? He started to sink. Peter was so busy worrying about the wind and the waves that he forgot all about Jesus. He forgot what he was supposed to stay focused on. So how can you keep your eyes on Jesus? Guess what? You are doing it right now! Whenever you take time to read about Jesus, whenever you pray, whenever you talk to him, you are focusing on Jesus. When you do those things, you are putting God first. And that is just what he wants you to do.

Believe!

✻

KEY IDEA:

I focus on God and his priorities for my life.

KEY VERSE:

Put God's kingdom first. Do what he wants you to do.
Then all those things will also be given to you.

—Matthew 6:33

CHAPTER 15

Total Surrender

ACT

The Key Question:
How do I grow a life of sacrificial service?

Have you ever heard of the word sacrifice*? A sacrifice is something we* choose *to do, even though we might not* want *to do it. When you choose to help your mom clean the house, even though you would rather go out and play, you are making a sacrifice. When you choose to give some of your money to the church, even though you would rather keep it, you are making a sacrifice.*

So when we ask the key question, How do I grow a life of sacrificial service? *what we really want to find out is,* How can I choose to live my life so that I do what God wants, instead of what I want? *Sacrifice means choosing God first and ourselves last. It is not easy. But let's find out what happened one day when Shadrach, Meshach, and Abednego chose to put God first.*

The Fiery Furnace
Daniel 3

For a long, long time Israel followed God and was a great nation. But gradually the people forgot about God, and Israel wasn't strong anymore. The nation was defeated by the Babylonians, and the people were taken away to the country of Babylonia. Now the Babylonian people and their king did not worship God.

One day, King Nebuchadnezzar ordered his workers to build a giant golden statue and put it in an open field where everyone could see it. The king made a law commanding everyone to bow down and worship the statue whenever they heard the king's special music. If someone didn't obey, the king would throw them into a blazing furnace to die.

But Shadrach, Meshach, and Abednego were Israelites who put God first. They refused to worship the statue. They would only worship the one true God, no matter what.

When the king heard that these young men broke his law, he was furious. He ordered they be thrown into the huge blazing hot furnace. But first he said, "Make the fire seven times hotter than usual!"

The king watched as the soldiers threw Shadrach, Meshach, and Abednego into the furnace. "Weren't only three men thrown into the fire?" asked the king. "I see four men, and one of them looks like a god!"

The king approached the furnace. "Shadrach, Meshach, Abednego!" he yelled. "Servants of the Most High God, come out of there!"

So the three young men walked out of the furnace. Nothing on them was burnt, and they didn't even smell of smoke!

"Your God is great!" cried the king. "He sent his angel to rescue you. From now on, no one will be allowed to say anything bad about your God."

The Jump to Jesus

Did you see how Shadrach, Meshach, and Abednego chose to put God first, and themselves last? Do you think they *wanted* to walk into that hot, fiery furnace? It must have been a very hard choice to make, but they were ready to sacrifice their lives for God.

When Jesus came to earth, he was ready to sacrifice his own life too. Jesus gave his life away. He put *us* first and himself last. Jesus told people, *If you really want to be my followers, you have to say no to yourself and yes to God. But if you lose your life for me you will save it.* Find out what Jesus meant in the story of one of his followers called Stephen.

Stephen's Story

Acts 6:8–7:60

After Jesus went to heaven, many people believed in him and were saved. But not everyone believed Jesus was the Son of God. Some people were angry with the new Christians and tried to hurt them.

Stephen was a man who became a member of the new church. He was filled with God's grace and power. In God's name, Stephen performed miracles. But some members of the synagogue didn't like Stephen. They tried to prove that what Stephen said about Jesus was wrong. But Stephen kept telling them the wonderful news about Jesus.

Stephen's enemies decided to make up stories about him that weren't true. They knew Stephen would be in big trouble if they said he was speaking against Moses and God.

The men lied to anyone who would listen. "Stephen says bad things about Moses and God," they said.

The teachers of the Jewish people believed the bad men. They brought Stephen before the officials. They asked Stephen to explain himself.

But Stephen didn't talk about himself. Instead, he talked about what God had done for his people. He told them the old stories of Abraham, Isaac, Jacob, and Joseph. He reminded them that Moses long ago spoke about a prophet who was coming. He told them that Joshua, David, and Solomon all listened to God. He told them how Solomon built the temple for God. And he told the men that time after time people made bad choices against God.

Stephen said, "You people are so stubborn. You won't listen! You don't want the Holy Spirit. You've killed the men of God who told us that Jesus was coming. You know God's law, but you don't keep it."

When the officials heard this, they became very angry.

But Stephen was filled with the Holy Spirit. He saw the glory of God. He pointed to the sky. "Look, I can see the heavens opening up. I can see Jesus standing at the right hand of God."

The officials covered their ears and chased Stephen out of the city. Then the crowd picked up stones and threw them at Stephen. He was badly hurt. "Lord Jesus, receive my spirit!" he cried. Stephen fell down on his knees. "Lord, do not hold this sin against them!" Then Stephen died and went to heaven to be with Jesus.

THE
JESUS ANSWER

Did you notice how Stephen chose God first and himself last? And because Stephen believed in God, he did not really lose his life—he saved it! Stephen went to a far more wonderful life in heaven. So how can you sacrifice? How can you live your life so that you do what God wants, instead of what you want?

Jesus would tell you to choose God first. Don't just do what you want to do. Check in with God every day, and ask him what he wants you to do. Say yes to God. And if you can do those things you will be living for God. And that is the very best life there is.

Believe!

✳

KEY IDEA:

I dedicate my life to God's plan.

KEY VERSE:

When you offer your bodies to God, you are worshiping him in the right way.

—Romans 12:1

CHAPTER 16

Biblical Community

ACT

The Key Question:
How do I develop healthy relationships with others?

Imagine you're standing in a very big circle with lots of people. There are moms and dads, boys and girls, grandmas and grandpas, people from all over the world. Everyone in the circle is holding hands because they love each other. They work together and share what they have. They laugh together and help each other. And right in the middle of the circle is the most important person. Can you guess who it is? That person is God.

What you imagined is what God's family looks like. It's called God's community. It is one where we hold hands, love each other, and put God right in the middle. And when we do that, we can do some wonderful things together. Let's find out what happened when one community worked together on a very special project.

Rebuilding the Wall of Jerusalem
Nehemiah 2:11–4:23; 6:15

For a long time, the people of Israel lived in another country. Finally, God told them it was time to go back home. Thousands of people returned to the land of Israel.

Then God told a man named Nehemiah to see what was happening in the city of Jerusalem. God said to Nehemiah, "Go around the outside of the city and take a look at the broken down wall. Find out what needs to be done to rebuild it." Nehemiah listened to God. He went to Jerusalem and did what God said.

After Nehemiah finished his inspection of the city wall, he called everyone together. He told the leaders of the city and the priests that Jerusalem was a mess. "We're in trouble," he said. "The gates are charred from fire. The walls have been torn down. The stones from the walls are piled up like trash. We have to join together and rebuild the walls around Jerusalem. God told me to come and do this. He will be with us."

The people heard Nehemiah and believed him. Everyone in the Jewish community agreed to rebuild a part of the wall. The priests rebuilt the wall and the gate near the temple. Each official selected a section near their homes and rebuilt it. Those who worked with gold or made perfume repaired the wall in front of their shops. Even the noblemen repaired a section of the wall. Rich people and poor people, men and women, old people and children helped to rebuild the miles of wall and the ten gates that surrounded the city of Jerusalem.

But the enemies of the Jewish people laughed and made fun of the workers. They threatened to hurt Nehemiah and the builders.

Nehemiah told the people, "Don't be afraid. Remember—God is great and awesome. He won't let us fail." So everyone continued to work together.

The people rebuilt together from one end of Jerusalem's wall to the other. They hung the gates and replaced the roofs. They placed stone on top of stone to make the wall strong. The people worked as a community on every section of the wall and the gates without stopping. With God's help, they finished the wall of Jerusalem in fifty-two days.

The Jump to Jesus

Did you see what happened when everyone in the community worked together? The huge wall of Jerusalem was rebuilt in just fifty-two days! Now do you know why they were able to get that important project done so fast? It was because they put God at the center of their team, and they all helped each other.

When Jesus came to earth, he reminded people how to live in community, as God's family. He told them to put God in the very middle of their lives and to love and serve others. And in case they didn't understand how to do that, Jesus showed them. One day, he even knelt down and washed his disciples' dirty feet. Jesus wanted people to know how important it is to care for each other. After Jesus went back to heaven, the first church in Jerusalem did just that. As you read this story, see if you can spot all the different ways this community of believers cared for each other.

A Community of Believers

Acts: 2:42–47; 4:32–37

When Jesus returned to heaven, he sent the Holy Spirit to be with his disciples. The disciples told others about Jesus. They told people that Jesus died for their sins. They talked about Jesus' gifts of love and grace. They performed miracles and baptized the new believers.

The people listened and were amazed. They felt God's love. They told other people about God's love and forgiveness. And every day the community of believers grew larger. The believers were happy. They loved each other, and they loved Jesus.

Soon they realized they wanted to be together all the time. So they shared everything they had. They shared their food, their houses, and their clothes. No one had to worry about anything. They took care of each other. During the day they listened to teachings about Jesus. When evening came they had supper together. All the believers praised God by singing songs together.

THE JESUS ANSWER

Did you notice all the different ways those people cared for each other? And did you see how they opened their arms wide to welcome new people? That is just like our circle of people growing bigger and bigger as we ask others to join our community of believers. So what do we do to develop healthy relationships with others? We love and care for each other as sisters and brothers. We work together to do wonderful things for God. We share and help each other. And most importantly, we keep God right in the center of it all—because that is where he belongs.

Believe!

✳

KEY IDEA:

I spend time with other Christians to accomplish God's plan in my life, in the lives of others, and in the world.

KEY VERSE:

All the believers were together. They shared everything they had.

—Acts 2:44

CHAPTER 17

Spiritual Gifts

ACT

The Key Question:
What gifts and skills has God given me to serve others?

What are you good at? Are you good at soccer or gymnastics? Maybe you're good at painting or reading or swimming. Everyone is good at something. That's the way God made us. But did you know God also gives us "spiritual gifts"? These are special gifts that come from the Holy Spirit. They are things like teaching, helping, serving, giving, or encouraging others. God wants us to discover what gifts and skills we have. Then we can use those skills to serve the people around us and help others come to know God.

Do you remember the story of Daniel, who was thrown into the den of lions? He was someone who used the gifts God gave him to help others. In this new story, he helps King Nebuchadnezzar. Let's find out what happened …

Daniel Interprets the King's Dream
Daniel 2:1–47

King Nebuchadnezzar was the king of the Babylonian Empire, the largest country in the world. To make his kingdom so big, Nebuchadnezzar ordered his army to march into other countries. The army even invaded Israel and took God's people away to the city of Babylon.

One night, King Nebuchadnezzar had a strange dream about a giant statue. In the morning, he wanted to know what it meant. So he asked his wise men, "If you are so smart, tell me about the dream I had and what it means."

The wise men said it was impossible to do what the king asked.

King Nebuchadnezzar was furious. He ordered all the wise men of Babylon to be killed. But one wise man named Daniel asked for time to figure out the dream.

Daniel was one of God's people whom the king had captured. He worked for the king, but he obeyed God. That night, Daniel went home and prayed to God for help. God gave Daniel a vision explaining King Nebuchadnezzar's dream. Daniel thanked God and said:

"Praise be to the name of God forever
He gives wisdom to the wise.
I thank and praise you, God of my ancestors:
You have given me wisdom and power,
you have made known to me what we asked of you,
you have made known to us the dream of the king."

Daniel returned to King Nebuchadnezzar and told him, "I am not smarter than everyone else. God told me your dream and gave me its meaning in a vision." Then Daniel told King Nebuchadnezzar what his strange dream meant.

King Nebuchadnezzar said, "Your God is the God of gods and the Lord of kings. He reveals mysteries, for you were able to reveal this mystery to me."

The Jump to Jesus

Did you notice what happened when Daniel used the gift God had given him to explain the king's dream? King Nebuchadnezzar realized no one was greater than God! Daniel was able to show King Nebuchadnezzar what God is like.

When we use our spiritual gifts to serve others, we can do the same. We can show others what God is like. Jesus talked a lot about spiritual gifts. He told his disciples it was important for them to find out what God had made them good at and then use those skills to help others. One day, that's what Peter did.

Peter Heals a Crippled Man

Acts 3:1–10

One day, after Jesus had gone back to heaven, Peter and John went to the temple to pray. When they reached the gate leading into the temple, they saw a man who couldn't walk. Each day this man's friends would place him by the temple gate to beg for money.

"Please," begged the man. "Can you help the poor?"

Peter and John both stopped.

"Look at us," said Peter. "I do not have any silver or gold. But I do have this." Then Peter bent down, took the man's hand, and said, "In the name of Jesus Christ, I say to you, rise up and walk!"

147

The man leaped to his feet in joy! He went with them to the temple, walking and jumping and praising God all the way. Everyone who had known this man stared in wonder.

THE
JESUS ANSWER

How wonderful that Peter used his spiritual gift of healing to make that crippled man better. And how happy that man was to be able to walk and run and jump. Now he knew how wonderful God is! As you grow up, find out what God made you good at. Once you know, don't keep it to yourself. Use your gifts and skills to serve others. When all God's people do that, it becomes a beautiful picture of God at work in the world. And everyone around us will see what a wonderful God we have!

Believe!

❋

KEY IDEA:

I know my spiritual gifts and use them to bring about God's plan.

KEY VERSE:

We all have gifts. They differ according to the grace God has given each of us.

—Romans 12:6

CHAPTER 18

Offering My Time

ACT

The Key Question: How do I best use my time to serve God and others?

Just imagine how God would feel if everyone in the whole world woke up in the morning, jumped out of bed, and said, Good morning, God. How do you want me to use my time today? God would be so happy! And the world would be a happier place too. People would help each other more, they would listen to each other, and they would listen to God. But it can be hard to give all our time to God.

Sometimes, God has to remind us to do that. Sometimes God has to say, It's time to listen to me. It's time to do what I want you to do. One day, God told Haggai to bring that same message to the people of Israel when they had stopped working on a very important project.

God's People Finish Building the Temple

Haggai 1:1–15

For a long, long time, God's people lived in another country, far away from the city of Jerusalem. Finally, they returned to the city, but it had been destroyed. God's temple was a pile of burned wood and broken stones. So the people gathered together and started to rebuild God's house. After a while, they got tired of the project and stopped. Many years passed, and the temple was still not finished.

God told the prophet Haggai to give a message to the king and the people. "Tell them to think about what they've been doing all these years," God said. "Tell them they have it all wrong. They have not used their time wisely. They built beautiful houses for themselves, but they forgot about me. They forgot about taking the time to build my house. It remains a pile of burnt wood and stone. They made the foundation for my new temple, but then they stopped and took care of themselves. This is not right. It is time to finish my house."

The king and the people listened to Haggai's message because they knew God had sent him. They loved God and wanted to follow what he said. Haggai told the people, "God wants you to know that he is with you."

Then God made the leaders and the people eager and excited to finish building the temple. All the people went up into the mountains. They cut down trees for lumber. They brought the wood back to the city. Then they finished building God's house.

The Jump to Jesus

Do you remember what the people were building instead of building God's house? They were building beautiful houses for themselves. They forgot about God. That was not a smart way to use their time. And that's why God sent Haggai—to remind them to be wise and to use their time in the way God wanted.

But someone who never needed to be reminded about using time wisely was Jesus. Even when Jesus was a young boy, he was wise. Jesus knew how important it was to listen to God, to learn from him, and to use his time in just the way God wanted. Let's learn about how Jesus did that in the next story.

Jesus in His Father's House
Luke 2:41–52

When Jesus was twelve years old, he went on a trip. He traveled with his family from their home in Nazareth to Jerusalem. They made this trip every year during the Feast of Passover. Then, when the celebration in the city was over, Jesus' family gathered and began their journey home.

But that year, Jesus remained in Jerusalem without his parents knowing it. After some time, Mary and Joseph realized Jesus was missing. Frightened, Mary and Joseph returned to Jerusalem to look for him.

For three days they searched the streets. Finally, they found Jesus in the temple. He was listening and speaking with the teachers. All who heard Jesus were amazed at his understanding of God's Word.

Mary said, "Jesus, we have been so worried! Why did you stay here?"

Jesus looked at his mother and said, "Didn't you know I needed to be in my Father's house?"

Mary and Joseph didn't understand Jesus' words.

Jesus returned home to Nazareth with his parents and he became stronger and wiser.

THE
JESUS ANSWER

Imagine how worried Mary and Joseph must have been when Jesus was missing for three days. But Jesus was not wasting his time. When he stayed behind in the temple, Jesus was using his time wisely—to learn more about God and how God wanted him to live. As Jesus grew up, he talked with God, and asked God to show him how to use his time. So how can you *best use your time to serve God and others? Try to be like Jesus. Start tomorrow! In the morning, jump out of bed and say,* Good morning, God. How do you want me to use my time today? *And God, who is always listening, will show you how to live.*

Believe!

✳

KEY IDEA:
I offer my time to help God's plan.

KEY VERSE:
Do everything you say or do in the name of the Lord Jesus.

—Colossians 3:17

CHAPTER 19

Giving My Resources

ACT

The Key Question:
How do I best use my resources to serve God and others?

Do you know the word resources? *Resources are everything we have— our healthy bodies, our homes, our clothes, our toys, our time, our money, and even what we do really well. So when we ask the question,* How do I best use my resources to serve God and others? *what we want to find out is,* How can I use everything God has given me to please him and help others?

Do you remember learning about God's special family called the Israelites? For a long time, the Israelites had no home. They traveled through the desert to a new land that God had promised them. While they were in the desert, God told them to build him a very special place, called a tabernacle, *so he could be with them. This wasn't easy. As you read this next story, see if you can spot all the different resources the Israelites gave to build God's tabernacle.*

Gifts for the Tabernacle

Exodus 35:4–29; 36:1–6

Moses called all the Israelite community together. "We are going to build a tabernacle for the Lord," he said. "Everyone take some of the things that you have and offer them to God. Bring your gold, silver, and bronze. We also need yarn, linen, animal skins, wood, olive oil, spices, and gems. All of these materials will be used to build a sanctuary for the tabernacle.

"If you are skilled as a builder, a seamstress, a metal worker, or a jeweler, offer your services. We'll need all of you to build a tabernacle for the Lord."

Then all the people who were willing brought their offerings of gold and silver and bronze. They gave yarn and fabric, animal skins and wood, olive oil and spices and jewels. They all gave because they wanted to.

Then the people with skills gathered and began the work. Each one volunteered his or her talents. Every day more offerings were given. Finally, Moses had to tell people they had given more than enough materials. And they built the sanctuary just as the Lord commanded.

The Jump to Jesus

Wow! Can you remember all the different gifts the Israelites brought to Moses? How amazing that everyone was so generous and put all their resources together to build God's tabernacle.

Many, many years after the tabernacle was made, some other people traveled across the desert. But these people were not Israelites. They were wise men who had been studying the stars at night. And do you know what they found out? They found out that a very special king had been born. You probably know who that was, don't you? It was Jesus! Now, what gift would you give to a king? Wouldn't you want to bring him the very best gift you could? That is just what the wise men did. They chose their finest gifts, jumped on their camels, and set off on a wonderful adventure to find the new king …

The Wise Men Visit Jesus
Matthew 2:1–12

When Jesus was born in Bethlehem, some very wise men from the east saw a bright new star in the sky. They decided to take a trip and follow the star. It led them to Jerusalem. They went to King Herod and asked, "Where is the newborn king of the Jews?"

King Herod didn't know about Jesus' birth. He called all of his priests and scribes together and asked, "Where is the Savior going to be born?" The priests and scribes answered, "The prophets say he is to be born in Bethlehem of Judea."

Herod told the wise men, "Go to Bethlehem and search for the child. Send for me when you find him. I want to go and worship him too."

The wise men left Jerusalem. Again, the star they had followed rose and moved across the sky ahead of them. It led them to the house where Jesus was with his mother, Mary.

The wise men bowed down and worshiped Jesus. They gave him magnificent treasures of gold, incense, and myrrh. When they left, the wise men were warned in a dream not to return to Herod because Herod wanted to harm Jesus. So they took a different route back to their country.

THE
JESUS ANSWER

The wise men were very generous to give their magnificent treasures to Jesus. Now maybe you don't have any silver or gold, but did you know that everyone *has treasures they can give? Our time, our money, what we do really well—these are all treasures we can give. So be ready to share toys, give hugs, and love everyone. When you live like that—when you are generous and giving—you are using your resources to serve God and others.*

Believe!

❋

KEY IDEA:

I give my resources to help God's plan.

KEY VERSE:

Make sure that you also do well in the grace of giving to others.

—2 Corinthians 8:7

CHAPTER 20

Sharing My Faith

ACT

The Key Question:
How do I share my faith with those who don't know God?

Did you know there are lots and lots of people in the world who don't know God? They don't know how he created our beautiful world, how he watches over his people, or how much he loves them. And so God wants us to do something special—he wants us to tell others about how wonderful he is.

When we tell someone about God, it is called sharing our faith. But sharing our faith is not always easy. And sometimes it can be scary. Read what happened when God asked Jonah to go to a place called Nineveh to tell others about him.

Jonah Tells Other People about God

Jonah 1–4

Jonah was a prophet. His job was to give people messages from God. One day, God told Jonah, "Go to Nineveh. Tell the people to behave. They are breaking my laws."

Jonah didn't want to do what God said. He knew that Nineveh was a bad place. The whole city was evil. So Jonah ran away and found a boat sailing away from Nineveh. *I will hide from God on this ship*, he thought.

But God saw Jonah. He was angry Jonah hadn't done what he asked. God sent a terrible storm to toss the ship.

The sailors cried, "What have we done to anger the gods?"

Jonah told them, "You haven't done anything. This storm is my fault. I made God very angry. I tried to run away from him. I didn't want to do what he asked me to do."

"What shall we do?" asked the sailors.

"Throw me overboard," said Jonah. "Then you will be safe."

The sailors threw Jonah into the fierce waves. The sea was instantly calm. The men saw how strong and powerful Jonah's God was, and they worshiped him.

God sent a big fish to swallow Jonah. For three days and nights, Jonah sat in the belly of the great fish. He had a lot of time to think about what he had done. He prayed to God for forgiveness.

God forgave Jonah. He commanded the fish to spit Jonah out. The fish did exactly what God asked. And the waves washed Jonah up on the shore. Again, God said to Jonah, "Tell the people of Nineveh to change their ways."

Jonah went straight to Nineveh and warned the people. They were sorry for breaking God's Laws. God forgave them.

The Jump to Jesus

Did you see what happened when Jonah was brave and went to share his faith in Nineveh? All the people in the city decided to listen to God. How happy God must have been that day.

The Bible is full of stories about people who shared their faith so that others would know about God. Some people who believed in Jesus shared their faith just by the way they lived. They were kind, they helped others, and they shared everything they had. Other people traveled many miles in every direction to tell people the good news about Jesus. Philip was one person who shared his faith in this way.

Philip Shares the Bible with a Man from Ethiopia

Acts 8:26–40

After Jesus went back to heaven, the first church started in Jerusalem. Philip was a member of the church. He was filled with the Holy Spirit and began to tell others about Jesus. One day, an angel of the Lord talked to Philip. The angel told Philip to leave Jerusalem and travel south on the desert road. So Philip did.

On the road, he met a man from Ethiopia. The Ethiopian was an officer in charge of the queen's treasury. He had come to Jerusalem to worship God.

Philip heard the Ethiopian reading God's Word and asked him, "Do you understand what you are reading?"

The Ethiopian shook his head no. "I need someone to explain it to me," he said. So the Ethiopian invited Philip to sit with him in his chariot. He asked Philip, "Who is the prophet Isaiah talking about when he talks about a lamb?"

Philip explained, "Jesus was the lamb killed for our sins. Jesus died and rose again from the dead so we could have eternal life. You can have eternal life too if you believe in Jesus and accept him as your savior."

As they traveled along, the Ethiopian asked Philip to baptize him. They stopped when they saw some water. Philip baptized the Ethiopian who believed in Jesus. Then the Ethiopian went on his way rejoicing.

THE
JESUS ANSWER

Because Philip was ready to share his faith, a wonderful thing happened—the Ethiopian man believed in Jesus and was baptized. So how can you share your faith with those who don't know God? Maybe you could read your Bible with a friend, like Philip did. Maybe you could show others what it means to follow Jesus by being kind, generous, and helpful. Or maybe you could tell your friends about God and how much he loves you.

If you can do those things, you will be like a light shining in the world for Jesus. More and more people will come to know God, and that will be a wonderful thing.

Believe!

✤

KEY IDEA:
I share my faith with others to help God's plan.

KEY VERSE:
Pray that I will be bold as I preach the good news.

—Ephesians 6:20

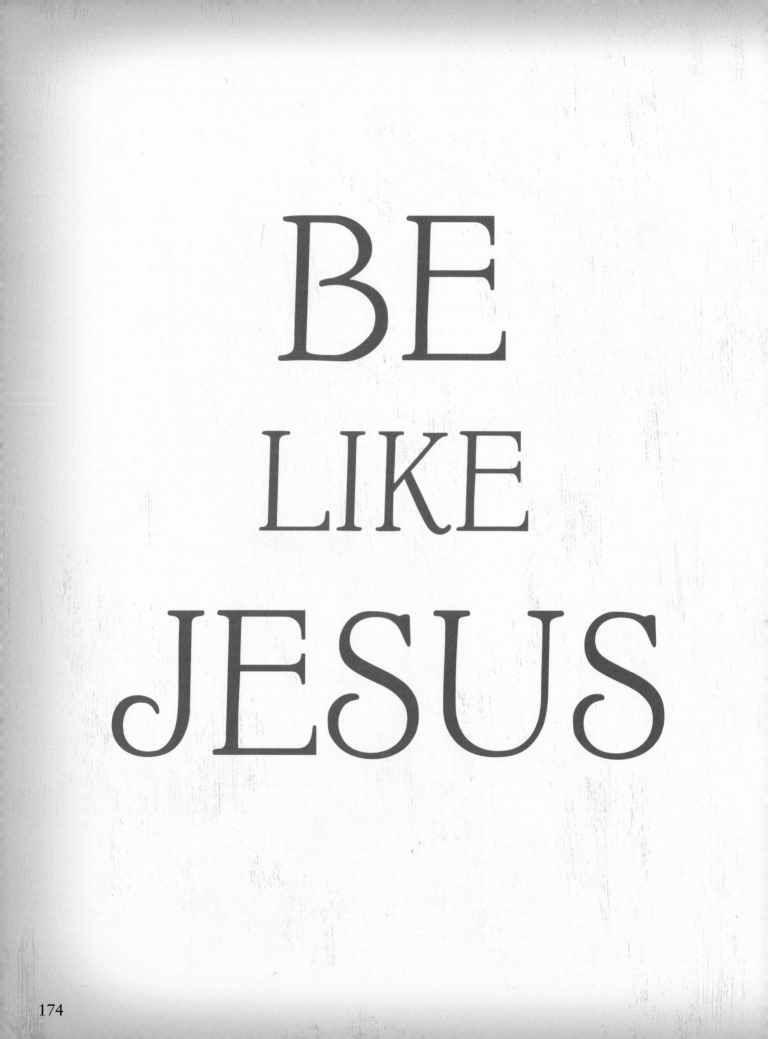

BE
LIKE
JESUS

CHAPTER 21

Love

BE

The Key Question:
What does it mean to sacrificially, unconditionally love others?

There are some big words in our question for today. *What does it mean to sacrificially, unconditionally love others?* These words mean that we try to love others as much as we love ourselves—or even more. But how do we do that?

We'll find the answer in the Bible—because the Bible is a book about love. From the very first page to the very last, the Bible tells the wonderful story of the love God has for his people. Through the stories of the Bible, we learn that God wants us to love him and love others. The Bible tells us that love begins with God. God fills us up with his love so that we can love those around us. Let's find out more about this special kind of love in one of the most beautiful stories in the Bible. It's a story about two friends named David and Jonathan.

Old Testament

David and Jonathan
1 Samuel 18:1-4; 19:1-7; 20:1–42

God's people settled in the Promised Land. After many years, the people asked God to give them a king. So God appointed Saul to be the first king of Israel. Saul had a son named Jonathan and a military helper named David. David and Jonathan were friends. They swore to be friends forever in the name of the Lord.

One day, David went to his friend. He asked Jonathan why his father, King Saul, was trying to kill David.

Jonathan couldn't believe that King Saul would want to hurt David. But David convinced him it was true. Jonathan loved his friend, so he asked him how he could help.

David said, "Tomorrow is the New Moon Festival. Go to dinner with your father the king. Listen to what he says about me. Find out if the king has a plan to kill me. If he does, promise me you'll come and warn me. I'll wait in the field until you come and tell me the news." Jonathan promised to warn David.

The next night, King Saul asked Jonathan why David wasn't at the festival. Jonathan lied to the king to protect David. He made up a story to explain why David wasn't at the table for dinner. King Saul got angry. He called Jonathan a traitor. And he yelled, "David must die!" Then he threw a spear at Jonathan.

Right away, Jonathan knew his father wanted to kill David so he left the festival.

The next day, Jonathan went to the field to find David. He told David, "You must run away. You aren't safe here. My father wants to kill you." David and Jonathan cried together. They didn't know if they would ever see each other again. They left each other knowing their friendship would never die.

The Jump to Jesus

Did you see how Jonathan loved David as much as he loved himself? Jonathan was ready to die to save David from King Saul. He was ready to give up his own life to save his friend. That is called sacrificial love.

Does that remind you of someone else? Does that remind you of Jesus? Jesus was ready to give up his life for us. Jesus told his disciples, I am the good shepherd . . . the good shepherd gives his life for the sheep. As you read this next story, try to imagine Jesus like a good shepherd, loving you and taking care of you—his little sheep.

New Testament

A Good Shepherd Loves His Sheep

John 10:11–18

Jesus performed many miracles and told stories to the people. Jesus wanted them to understand that he loved them and he would take care of them.

Jesus compared himself to a shepherd who watches over and cares for his sheep. Just imagine what would happen if sheep didn't have a shepherd. One of the sheep might wander off and get lost or hurt or even eaten by a wild animal! Jesus knew people were a lot like sheep, so he told them this story:

"I am the good shepherd. The good shepherd gives his life for the sheep.

"The hired worker is not like the shepherd. He does not own the sheep, so he does not care about them. When he sees the wolf coming, he leaves the sheep alone and runs away. Then the wolf attacks the flock and the sheep scatter.

"The man runs away because he just gets paid to do this job. He doesn't care about the sheep enough to risk his life for them.

"But I am the good shepherd; I know my sheep and my sheep know me. I love my sheep and I am willing to give my life for them. I have other sheep that don't belong to this group. I want to bring them into my flock. They too will listen to my voice, and there shall be one flock and one shepherd.

"The reason my Father loves me is that I love my sheep and will give my life for them."

When Jesus finished his story, some people did not understand what Jesus was trying to explain. But others understood he was the Son of God, our Savior, and the way to eternal life.

THE
JESUS ANSWER

Can you see the picture in your mind of Jesus taking care of you? Can you feel the wonderful love he has for you? Jesus helps us find the answer to our question. To sacrificially and unconditionally love others means that we try to love like Jesus. We forgive. We are patient. We are kind. We try to love others as much as we love ourselves. We take all the love God gives us and share it with everyone we meet.

Believe!

✺

KEY IDEA:
I will try hard to love God and love others.

KEY VERSE:
Since God loved us this much, we should also love one another.

—1 John 4:11

CHAPTER 22

Joy

BE

The Key Question:
What gives us true happiness and contentment in life?

What makes you happy? What fills your heart with happiness, cheerfulness, and joy? Do you feel happy when it's your birthday or when you have fun with your family? Maybe you feel happy when you get a present or when you play with your friends. God loves it when we are happy. But there's so much more to true happiness than enjoying our birthday, or getting presents, or having a good time. Real joy and happiness come from knowing God and remembering how much he loves us.

In Old Testament times, God's people gathered together to celebrate his goodness. Knowing God took care of them over and over again filled them with joy and happiness. See how the people in this next story celebrated as they remembered how God had helped them.

Celebrating the Joy of the Lord
Nehemiah 8:1–18

Israel's enemies had destroyed God's temple and burned it. They captured the people and took them far away to another country. After many years, God's people returned to Jerusalem. They rebuilt the city and God's temple.

In the fall, all the Israelites gathered together in the area near the city gate. The men, women, and children asked Ezra to read from the Law of Moses.

Ezra, a teacher of the law, stood on a special wooden platform so all the people could see him. He opened the scroll. Then he praised God. The people stood up and raised their hands high and said, "Amen!" Ezra read from the Book of the Law for hours.

The leaders of the temple explained to the people the meaning of what they heard. Soon the people understood what God said in the Book of the Law. Many people began to cry. They felt bad because they hadn't followed the rules God had given them.

But the leaders said to the people, "Don't cry. This is a special day. Don't be sad, for the joy of the Lord is your strength. Go and enjoy special food, and drink sweet drinks. Share your food with others. It is a day to be joyful!"

The teachers told the Israelites, "According to the Law, God wants us to remember when he freed us from slavery in Egypt and we lived in tents in the wilderness. Go outside the city and gather branches. Build your family a small hut. Eat your meals and sleep in the hut during the celebration."

The people went out into the hills and cut down branches from the olive trees. They gathered palm branches and boughs from the myrtle trees. Then they built their huts on the roofs of their houses, in their courtyards, or in a city square. For seven days, Ezra read from the Law of God and all the people listened. They lived in their huts and celebrated. And they were full of joy.

The Jump to Jesus

What a joyful time that was as the Israelites listened to God's Word and remembered how he took care of them.

In the New Testament, one of the most joyful times was the night Jesus was born. God's angels came from heaven with the most wonderful news the world had ever heard. They came to some shepherds on the hillsides of Bethlehem. It was a night the shepherds would never forget.

Angels Give the Shepherds Joyful News

Luke 2:1–20

When it was almost time for Jesus to be born, Joseph and Mary traveled to Bethlehem. But when they got there, they couldn't find a place to stay. An innkeeper felt sorry for the weary travelers and offered them the use of his stable. That night, Mary gave birth to her son. She wrapped him in cloth and placed him in a manger filled with soft hay.

Near the town, shepherds were caring for their sheep on a hillside. Suddenly an angel appeared in front of them. "Don't be afraid," said the angel. "God has sent me to tell you the greatest news. It will bring joy to everyone. This very day, a Savior is born in the city of David! You will find him wrapped in cloths and sleeping in a manger."

Then the night burst into brilliant light and angels filled the sky. "Glory to God!" they sang. "Peace on earth! Good will to all people!"

The shepherds said, "Let's go see what's happened!" They left the hillside and went down to Bethlehem. And just as the angel had said, they found baby Jesus sleeping in a manger.

THE
JESUS ANSWER

Can you imagine how happy those shepherds felt when they found baby Jesus? They truly did find joy that day. And guess what? Jesus still brings joy to everyone who knows him. Knowing God and his son Jesus is what makes us happy. Think about it—God loves you! He has a marvelous plan for your life. God is with you every single day. You can count on him. When you know these wonderful things, you'll be filled with joy no matter what happens. The joy that comes from Jesus will be in you, *and no one will ever be able to take it away.*

Believe!

❋

KEY IDEA:
No matter what happens, I feel happy inside and understand God's plan for my life.

KEY VERSE:
I have told you this so that you will have the same joy that I have.

—John 15:11

Peace

BE

The Key Question:
Where do I find strength to battle worry and fear?

Have you ever felt worried or afraid? Being afraid is not a good feeling. God doesn't want us to feel afraid. He wants us to feel peace. Peace is a wonderful feeling. When we are filled with peace, we feel calm and restful inside. We are not worried. We are not afraid.

Because God is a God of peace, he wants us to live in peace with him, with others, and with ourselves. So how can we do that? Let's start by reading about King Solomon. When Solomon became king of God's people, God gave the people a long time of peace. They lived happily with one another and the nations around them.

Solomon's Kingdom at Peace

1 Kings 3:1–15, 4:20–25

After King David died, Solomon became king of Israel and Judah. He was a good leader who worshiped God. Every day Solomon prayed. He followed the laws given from God. And he built a temple for the Lord where the people could worship.

King Solomon wanted his kingdom to live in peace. So he made friends with all the kingdoms around him. Solomon and the king of Egypt decided they wanted to be friends. King Solomon married the daughter of the king of Egypt. He brought her home with him to live in Jerusalem.

One night, God spoke to Solomon in a dream. "Ask for anything you want. I will give it to you."

King Solomon could have asked for anything. He could have asked for gold, power, and so much more, but he didn't. Solomon thanked God for all he had. Then the king asked for a heart that could tell right from wrong.

God was pleased with King Solomon's choice. So God gave Solomon the gift of wisdom. He also made Solomon very rich and powerful. King Solomon ruled over a very big kingdom. The people had plenty to eat and drink. They were safe and lived in their own homes. They had grapevines and fig trees, fields of grain, barley, and hay. They had sheep and goats, deer and antelope, and birds to eat. They had plenty of crops and animals to provide for the kingdom's needs. Everyone had more than enough of everything.

God's people were happy and lived in peace while Solomon was king.

The Jump to Jesus

Can you see how Solomon lived in peace with God and others? Solomon had a wonderful relationship with God. He prayed, worshiped, and thanked God for everything he had. He made friends with all the kingdoms around him and made sure that everyone in his kingdom lived in peace.

God will help us as *we* try to live in peace with others. God sent Jesus to show us how to be kind and generous, friendly, forgiving, patient, and loving. Did you know that Jesus is called the Prince of Peace? Whenever we feel worried or afraid, Jesus is the one who can bring us peace. And this is what Jesus taught his disciples one scary, stormy night on Lake Galilee.

Jesus Calms the Storm

Mark 4:35–41

Jesus had been teaching a large group of people. He was very tired at the end of the day. He told his disciples he wanted to leave the crowds. He wanted to go to the other side of the lake. Jesus and the disciples climbed into a boat. The disciples started rowing but Jesus fell asleep in the back of the boat.

A furious storm began in the middle of the night. The wind blew. The waves rose high. They tossed the boat from side to side. The rain pelted the disciples, stinging their skin. The waves crashed over the sides of the boat, filling the boat faster than the disciples could bail the water out. The disciples became afraid. They couldn't believe that Jesus kept sleeping.

Finally, the disciples woke Jesus. They asked him, "Why don't you care that we're all going to drown?"

Jesus stood up. He shouted to the storm and waves, "Peace, be still!" Right away the storm stopped. Then he asked his disciples, "Why are you afraid? Don't you have faith in me?"

The disciples saw that the winds had stopped. The sky was clear and the water calm. They asked each other, "Who is this man? Even the wind and the waves obey him. They become peaceful when he tells them to be quiet."

THE
JESUS ANSWER

Wow! How amazing that Jesus calmed those waves, just by reaching out his hand and speaking. Jesus brought peace to his disciples, and he can bring peace to us too. So where do we find strength to fight our worries and fears?

We can find strength in Jesus. Jesus says, Do not worry about your life. Trust God. He knows everything you need. God will take care of you. Remember that God wants us to live in peace. The next time you start to worry or feel afraid, talk to Jesus, and let Jesus give you the precious gift of his peace.

Believe!

✳

KEY IDEA:

I am not worried because I have found peace with God, peace with others, and peace with myself.

KEY VERSE:

Don't worry about anything ... God's peace will watch over your hearts and your minds.

—Philippians 4:6–7

CHAPTER 24

Self-Control

BE

The Key Question:
How does God free me from
sin and bad habits?

Imagine that you and your grandma made some yummy chocolate cookies. They smell so good. Grandma finally gives you one. It tastes so delicious that you ask for one more. But your grandma says no. Then she leaves the room. You look at the cookies on the plate. You have to make a choice. You could choose to take one cookie, because your grandma would never know. Or you could turn away and leave them alone. What would you do? I hope you would make the right choice.

When we make the right choice and turn away from sinning, or doing the wrong thing, it's called self-control. God doesn't want us to sin. He really wants us to have self-control. In the Old Testament, God chose a man named Samson to help God's people. As you read the story, see if Samson had self-control. Did he make the right choice or the wrong one?

Samson Loses Control
Judges 13–16

After the Israelites spent forty years in the desert, they were allowed to go into Canaan, which they called the Promised Land. But they needed leaders to guide them. So God sent them leaders called judges. One of these judges was Samson. He was born to serve God. God gave Samson a gift.

"Samson, you are special," God said. "I'll give you the gift of great strength. But you must control yourself and never cut your hair. Your strength will leave you if you cut your hair. You must keep it a secret."

Samson kept his secret and grew to be stronger than a lion. Samson was even stronger than a thousand men. But Samson had enemies who wanted to know his secret.

Eventually Samson fell in love with Delilah. Now Samson's enemies saw a way to find out his secret. They bribed Delilah and told her, "If you find out the secret to Samson's strength, we will give you a lot of money."

Delilah asked Samson to tell her the secret of his strength. Samson didn't want to tell her, so he lied. When Delilah found out, she was angry. "You tricked me!" she shouted. "If you really loved me, you would tell me."

Samson knew it was wrong to tell Delilah his secret, so he tricked her again. This time Delilah complained, "How can you say you love me when you won't tell me your secret?"

Samson loved Delilah, even though she didn't love God. He couldn't control himself to keep his secret, and he forgot his promise to God. Finally he told Delilah his secret—that he was strong because of his long hair. Delilah said, "Now I know you really love me. Come, put your head on my lap and take a nap."

Right away, Samson fell asleep. And Delilah broke his trust. She told Samson's enemies to cut his hair. When they did, Samson became weak. Samson's enemies tied him up and put him in jail.

But while he was in jail, Samson's hair began to grow. It grew and grew and grew.

One day, Samson's enemies said, "Let's bring Samson to the temple so we can make fun of him and his God." They brought Samson to the temple and tied him between two columns.

Samson called out to God, "Deliver me from my enemy. Strengthen me again so I can show my enemy your mighty power."

And God remembered his promise to Samson. He returned Samson's power to him for one last time. Samson pushed hard against the temple columns over and over until they broke and fell down, destroying the temple and everyone inside.

The Jump to Jesus

Did you notice how Samson lost his self-control? It's sometimes hard to make the right choice. But if we can let God be in control of us, then he will help us to do the right thing.

One day, Jesus told a story about a son who left his father's home and made some bad choices. Let's find out what the father did when the son decided to turn away from his sin and come back home.

The Lost Son

Luke 15:11–32

While Jesus was on earth, he told this story to the people.

A father had two sons. They worked together on a large farm. One day, the younger son came to his father. He asked his father for half of everything the family owned. The father gave him the money. Then the son packed up his stuff and left the farm. He went to a far-away country. He bought everything he ever wanted. He spent all his money. He made bad choices and broke God's laws.

One day, the son had nothing to eat and he didn't have money left to buy food. He was very hungry. He was ready to do anything to get some money and food. So he got a job feeding pigs. The pigs had food, but he didn't. No one gave him anything to eat.

One day, he realized his father always fed the people he hired to work on the farm. They were never hungry like he was. So the younger son decided to go home.

The father was really happy when he saw his son coming down the road to the house. He ran over to meet him. He gave him a big hug and kissed him.

The son said, "Father, I have sinned against you and God. Please let me work for you on the farm."

The father didn't answer. Instead he ordered the servants to make a big dinner to celebrate. He welcomed his son with fine clothes, jewels, and good food.

The older son came into the house from working in the fields. He saw the party for his brother and got angry. He asked his father why he hadn't ever had a party for him. The father told the older son that he could have a party anytime he wanted. The father said, "Your brother was lost and now he is found. He was dead and now he's alive."

THE
JESUS ANSWER

Did you see how happy the father was when his son turned away from his sins and came back home? That is how God feels when we turn away from sin too. Even when we make bad choices or make mistakes, God will still love us and welcome us back. So when you have to make a choice, think about what Jesus would want you to do. Obey your parents, think before you speak, say kind words, be ready to share, be gentle, and love others. These are all wonderful choices that will help you have self-control.

Believe!

❊

KEY IDEA:

I have the power through Jesus to control myself.

KEY VERSE:

We must control ourselves. We must do what is right.

—Titus 2:12

CHAPTER 25

Hope

BE

The Key Question:
How do I deal with the hardships and struggles of life?

Long, long ago, the Israelites faced one of the hardest times they had ever known. One scary day, their enemies marched into the city, captured the Israelites, and took them far, far away from their homes. They did not know if they would ever go back home. They needed hope! So they cried out to God. And do you know what God did? God whispered hope into their hearts.

God sent Isaiah, his messenger, with some wonderful promises for them. Isaiah told them to hold on to hope—God had not forgotten them! Here's how it happened.

Isaiah the Prophet Brings Hope

Isaiah 40

An enemy nation marched into Israel. The army broke down the city wall and burned the buildings. They took away the people of Israel to a faraway place. The Israelites suffered a long, long time. Then they complained to God.

"Where is our God?" they cried. God saw the Israelites' misery and sent words of comfort and hope through the prophet Isaiah.

Isaiah said, "Do not be afraid, Israel, because you have paid for your sins. You are now forgiven.

Shout to the world the good news! Tell everyone your God is coming!

He is coming to rule the world with power. He will bring along with him the people he has rescued. He will take care of his people like a shepherd takes care of the flock he loves.

Who can be compared to God?

He knows everything.

He created everything.

He sees everything.

Lift up your eyes and see your Creator!
Because of his strength,
not one of you is missing.
He is your God forever.

Hope in your Lord and you will not
be disappointed.

Your strength will be renewed.

You will soar like an eagle!"

The Jump to Jesus

Did you see how many wonderful promises God gave the Israelites? Every single promise brought them hope. God promised to take care of them like a shepherd takes care of his sheep. He said that he would rescue them and make them strong again. God told them that if they put their hope in him, they would not be disappointed. So what do you think happened? Do you think the Israelites ever went back to their homes? They did! Because when God says something will happen, it happens. When God makes a promise, God keeps it.

Many, many years later, an old man called Simeon was waiting to see if a promise God made would come true. God had promised Simeon that one day he would see Jesus. Simeon really hoped it would happen. And one day, it did …

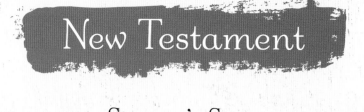

Simeon's Story

Luke 2:21–35

When Jesus was eight days old, Joseph and Mary took him to the temple in Jerusalem. They wanted to follow the Law of the Lord and present their firstborn son, Jesus, to God. They also brought a gift for God with them. They gave God an offering of two doves.

A man named Simeon lived in Jerusalem. The Holy Spirit was with him. Simeon hoped that one day he would see the Lord's Christ. He was told by the Holy Spirit that he wouldn't die until that happened.

One morning, Simeon was urged by the Holy Spirit to go to the temple. When he arrived at the temple, Simeon saw Joseph, Mary, and the baby Jesus. He held Jesus in his arms and praised God. "Lord, you can let me die now," he said. "What I hoped for has happened. I have seen your salvation."

Then Simeon told Mary and Joseph that Jesus was sent by God. Jesus was going to know people's hearts. Jesus was going to save many people. Mary and Joseph were amazed at the things Simeon said about their son.

THE
JESUS ANSWER

How wonderful that God kept his promise to Simeon. Simeon's story teaches us that God is not just a promise-maker—God is a promise-keeper! The most marvelous promise that God ever made was to send Jesus to the world. Jesus came to bring us hope, to remind us that God will never, ever leave us, and to show us that one day, we will be able to live with him forever. So how can you deal with the struggles and hardships of life? Trust in God and his wonderful promises. Let God whisper hope into your heart. You will never be disappointed.

Believe!

✳

KEY IDEA:
I can deal with the hardships of life because of the hope I have in Jesus.

KEY VERSE:

Our hope is certain … It is strong and secure.

—*Hebrews 6:19*

CHAPTER 26

Patience

BE

The Key Question:
How does God help me wait?

Have you ever stood in line for a really long time or waited your turn to play with a toy? It's no fun, is it? It can be hard to wait. But when we do that without complaining, it's called *patience*. When we're patient, we can stay calm. Did you know that God is really good at being patient? God does not get angry quickly. God is good at waiting.

God wants *us* to be good at waiting too. But how can we do that? We can learn from people in the Bible, like David, who had to be very patient and wait. Do you remember reading about King Saul and how he wanted to kill David? David escaped from Saul, but let's see what happened next, when Saul started to chase him.

David's Patience with King Saul

1 Samuel 24:1–22

King Saul was the first king of Israel. God had selected him to rule the people. Saul was a strong and powerful king, but he was jealous of a young man named David. He wanted David dead, and he spent many years chasing him all over the country.

One day, King Saul and his army followed David into the desert. When the king saw a dark cave, he went inside to rest.

217

David and his men were hiding deep in the back of the very same cave! David's men urged David to kill Saul while he had the chance. But David said to them, "God has selected Saul and anointed him king. I'll be patient and wait for God to decide when it's time for me to be king. I will not kill him." Instead, David snuck up on King Saul. He cut off a small piece of the king's robe without Saul knowing.

When Saul left the cave, David followed him. He called out to King Saul. Saul turned around and was shocked to see David. Then David bowed down in front of the king.

David told King Saul, "I was in the cave with you, but you didn't see me. I never wanted to harm you, but I could have. I came so close to you I was able to cut off the corner of your robe."

King Saul realized that David was a man of God. He was sorry he had tried to kill David. King Saul recognized that David would someday become king. He knew that the kingdom of Israel would become powerful under David's leadership.

The Jump to Jesus

How wise David was to wait for God's timing. If David had gotten angry, something terrible might have happened. But instead, David was patient. He did not get angry. Even though it was a very stressful time, he waited to see what God wanted him to do.

In the New Testament, someone else faced a stressful situation. This man had not been able to walk for a very long time. He had tried to get better for thirty-eight years! What a long time to wait. Let's find out what happened when he met Jesus.

Jesus Heals a Disabled Man

John 5:1–15

Jesus left Galilee to go to Jerusalem for a Jewish feast. As Jesus entered the city through the Sheep Gate he saw many disabled people. Some people couldn't see, and others couldn't walk. They sat near a pool named the Pool of Bethesda. They thought the water could make them better. Many people believed that angels stirred up the water in the pool. They also believed the first person who got into the pool when the water was stirred would be healed.

Jesus saw a man who was unable to walk. He knew the man had been crippled for many, many years. Jesus looked at the man and said, "Do you want to get well?"

The man thought Jesus was talking about being healed by the water in the pool. He said to Jesus, "I'm too slow to get to the pool when the angels stir up the water. I've been waiting a long time. Other people always get into the water before I can crawl close enough."

Jesus told the man, "Pick up your mat and walk." The man did what Jesus told him. Immediately, he stood up, picked up his mat, and walked around. The man was so happy! He told people that after thirty-eight years of being unable to walk, he was now healed! But when the man looked for Jesus, he was gone. Jesus had quietly slipped away into the crowd.

THE
JESUS ANSWER

How happy that man must have been when Jesus made his legs better. I bet he ran all the way home! At last, his stressful situation was gone.

So how does God provide the help you need to deal with stress? The next time you're angry, or upset, think about David or the man who couldn't walk. Think about how patient they were. You could try counting to five to help you be calm. And as you count, think about Jesus and what he would want you to do. If you can be patient and calm, even when things go wrong, everyone around you will notice. And you will not just be helping yourself— you will be helping others too.

Believe!

❋

KEY IDEA:
I do not get angry quickly, and I am patient, even when things go wrong.

KEY VERSE:
Anyone who is patient has great understanding.

—Proverbs 14:29

CHAPTER 27

Kindness/Goodness

BE

The Key Question:
What does it mean to do the right thing?

If you could peek into God's great big heart, do you know what you would see? You would see a wonderful heart that is kind and good. God wants our hearts to look like his. When we choose to be kind, it is always the right thing to do.

The Bible is full of stories about people who chose to be kind. Do you remember David's best friend, Jonathan? After Jonathan died, David thought about the promise he had made to Jonathan when they were young men. David had promised to be kind to Jonathan's family. Let's find out if David kept his promise.

David Shows Kindness to Jonathan's Son

2 Samuel 9:1–12

After King Saul died, David became the king of Israel. He was a good king. He wanted what was best for his people. One day, David asked if anyone in King Saul's family was still alive. He and King Saul's son, Jonathan, had been loyal friends. David wanted to honor that friendship by showing kindness to Jonathan's family.

One of the family servants told David that Jonathan's son, Mephibosheth, was still alive. The servant told David where he lived. He also told him that both of Mephibosheth's feet were hurt. Because of this, he had a hard time walking or working.

When King David met with Mephibosheth, Mephibosheth told David he would serve him any way he could. David gave him all the land and all the money that King Saul once owned. King David gave him servants to take care of the land. David always made sure that Mephibosheth's family and servants had everything they needed.

The Jump to Jesus

David didn't forget his promise to Jonathan. How kind of David to take care of Mephibosheth and be so generous with him. When Jesus came to earth, he often talked about being kind. He taught people to think carefully about how they treat others. He wanted everyone to find ways to be kind and good.

One day, Jesus went to eat at the home of a very important religious leader. A lot of other important people were there too. Jesus told them a story about what to do at a wedding dinner. He said that if they really wanted to be kind, they should invite other people as well as their friends. Who do you *think Jesus wanted them to invite? Let's find out if you're right …*

New Testament

Jesus Talks about Kindness
Luke 14:1–14

Jesus went to eat at a Pharisee's house on the Sabbath. Everyone there knew God's rule is that no one should work on the Sabbath. The Pharisees watched Jesus closely. They wanted to catch him doing something wrong.

Jesus noticed that a sick man was at the dinner. Jesus asked the Pharisees, "Is it against the law to heal a sick man on the Sabbath?" But they didn't answer.

When Jesus healed the man, the Pharisees were mad at him. Then Jesus asked the Pharisees, "If your son or your best ox fell into a well on the Sabbath would you pull them out?" Again they didn't answer Jesus.

Jesus saw that many of the guests rushed to the table to get the best seats. So he told them a story. "A man was invited to a wedding. When the man arrived, he took the best seat at the table. Later, the host asked the man to move to a lesser seat so someone more important could have his seat.

The man was embarrassed. Don't be like that selfish man. Instead be like the man who comes to the wedding and sits in the least important spot. Then the groom will come over and tell you to move to a much better seat, and everyone will notice that you have been honored. People who think they're important will be put down. People who don't act important will be lifted up."

229

Then Jesus gave the host of the dinner some advice. "Don't invite your family, your friends, or anyone who's rich to dinner. They will just pay you back with a dinner in return. Instead, give a dinner for the poor, the blind, and the disabled. They won't be able to pay you back, but God will see your kindness and reward you."

THE
JESUS ANSWER

Did you guess the right answer? Jesus wanted these folks to invite poor people to the big dinner. He wanted them to include blind people, hungry people, and people who couldn't care for themselves. Jesus teaches us that being kind to everyone is the right thing to do.

It's not always easy to do what Jesus asks. But as you grow up, try to be kind to everyone you meet. Perhaps if you see someone playing alone while you're playing with your friends, you could invite them to join you. Always look for ways you can be kind and good. When your heart is full of kindness and goodness, you will have a heart like God's.

Believe!

✻

KEY IDEA:

I choose to be kind and good in my relationships with others.

KEY VERSE:

Always try to be kind to each other and to everyone else.

—1 Thessalonians 5:15

CHAPTER 28

Faithfulness

BE

The Key Question:
Why is it important to be loyal and committed to God and others?

Everyone needs good friends. Good friends can be trusted. They won't let you down. They will stay with you and keep their promises. In other words, they are faithful. Now don't you think that sounds like God? God can be trusted. God won't let you down. God will stay with you, and he always keeps his promises. The Bible tells us that God's faithfulness is so great it can't be measured—it reaches all the way up to the skies! And because God is faithful to us, he wants us to be faithful to him and to others.

Near the beginning of God's story in the Bible, we hear about Abraham's great-grandson Joseph. There are many stories about Joseph. But whatever story we read, we learn that Joseph is a wonderful example of someone who was faithful to God, just as God was faithful to him.

God and Joseph: Faithful to One Another

From Genesis 37–45

Joseph was Jacob's favorite son. Jacob made Joseph a beautiful robe to wear. It was a robe made of many different colors. Joseph's brothers were jealous of his special robe. They were upset that Joseph was their dad's favorite. They were angry that Joseph was always bragging about himself.

"Let's get rid of him," the brothers said to each other. So one day when they were all out in the fields taking care of the sheep, they caught Joseph and threw him into a pit. Then they sold him to some traders as a slave. When the brothers went home, they lied to their father and told him, "Joseph has been eaten by wild animals." Jacob's heart was broken because he thought his son was dead.

But God was with Joseph. Even as a slave, Joseph was treated well by his master. Later, the master's wife lied about Joseph, and Joseph was thrown into jail.

Again, God was with Joseph. The jailer liked Joseph and put him in charge of the prisoners. One night, two prisoners had bad dreams.

With God's help, Joseph explained the dreams. Soon after that, Pharaoh, the king of Egypt, had a bad dream. He said, "Bring Joseph to me to explain my dream."

Joseph told Pharaoh, "With God's help I will tell you the meaning of your dream. Your dream is a warning. There will be seven years of good times and seven years of very bad times."

The pharaoh saw that God was with Joseph and that he was very wise. So Pharaoh put Joseph in charge of taking care of all the land and all the food in Egypt. During the good years, Joseph saved plenty of food so that when the bad times came there was enough food to save the people from going hungry.

Far away in Canaan, there wasn't any food saved, and Joseph's brothers were hungry. When they went to Egypt to get help, they met their long lost brother. They didn't know it was Joseph because he was all grown up. But Joseph recognized them and told them who he was.

The brothers remembered the terrible thing they had done to Joseph as a young boy. They shook in their sandals, afraid that Joseph would hurt them. But Joseph said, "I forgive you. I know that it was God's plan for me to come here and save all the people from going hungry. I'm glad to have my family back again."

The Jump to Jesus

What a hard life Joseph had. But did you notice how he stayed faithful to God and how God faithfully watched over him? Because Joseph never stopped trusting God, he was able to save his brothers and the whole nation of Israel from starving. Joseph's faithfulness brought about some good things—blessings.

In the New Testament, God called on a young girl named Mary to have faith and do something very special. He knew she could be a blessing to the whole world.

The Angel's Visit

Luke 1:26–38

When it was almost time for Jesus to come to earth, God sent the angel Gabriel to the town of Nazareth to speak to a young girl named Mary. Mary was engaged to Joseph, who was a relative of King David.

"Peace be with you, Mary!" Gabriel said. "The Lord is with you and has greatly blessed you."

Mary was surprised and afraid. "Don't be afraid, Mary," said Gabriel. "God thinks you are very special." Mary wondered what the angel's words meant.

"You are going to have a baby," the angel explained. "It will be a boy, and you will call him Jesus. He will be called the Son of the Most High God, and his kingdom will last forever."

Mary couldn't help but wonder, *How can this happen? I'm not married yet.*

The angel told her, "The Holy Spirit will come to you, and God's power will rest on you. For this reason, the child will be called the Son of God."

Trusting God, Mary replied, "I am the Lord's faithful servant. I believe that what you've said will really happen."

THE
JESUS ANSWER

Did you see how faithful Mary was when the angel told her she was going to be the mother of God's Son? Mary said, I am the Lord's servant. Let it happen. I'm sure God's heart filled with joy when he heard those words. What a wonderful blessing for Mary. Because of her faithfulness, Jesus, the King of the whole world, was born.

God is still calling out to his children. I think he's calling out to you. God says, Will you be faithful, like I am faithful to you? Can you be loyal and committed to me and others? I think you can. And when you say yes, you will be part of God's wonderful plan for the world, just like Mary was.

Believe!

✤

KEY IDEA:

I can be trusted because I keep my promises to God and others.

KEY VERSE:

Lord, your faithful love reaches up to the skies.

—Psalm 36:5

CHAPTER 29

Gentleness

BE

The Key Question:
How do I show thoughtfulness and consideration?

Are you thoughtful with others? If you wanted to play soccer, but your friend wanted to swing on the swings and talk, would you do what they wanted? If you did, that would be very thoughtful and gentle of you. When we consider others, when we think about their feelings and what they want, God is pleased.

Being gentle and thoughtful with people shows how much we love them. One day, David met two people, called Nabal and Abigail. As you read what happened in this story, try to remember all the different ways that Abigail was gentle.

Abigail Is Gentle with David

1 Samuel 25

When Saul was king of Israel, Nabal and his wife, Abigail, owned a large piece of property out in the country in Maon. Nabal was a wealthy man. He had thousands of sheep and goats. But Nabal was rude and mean to his servants and his wife, Abigail.

While running away from King Saul, David and his men traveled to Maon. David saw Nabal's shepherds and sheep out in the hills. He made sure the shepherds and the animals were safe from wild, hungry beasts and thieves.

When the time came for Nabal to clip the wool off the sheep, David sent ten men to speak to him and ask for his help. The men told Nabal about David's kindness to his shepherds. Then they asked Nabal for food and water for David's men.

Nabal said, "Who is this David? There are all kinds of servants running away these days. Why should I give food to these men from who knows where?"

So Nabal refused to help David's men. The men left empty-handed and returned to David. David was angry when he heard how Nabal had acted. He called his army together. He was going to kill Nabal and all of his men.

Abigail heard that her husband had shouted at David's men and sent them away. She quickly and quietly gathered food for David's troops. She collected loaves of bread, raisin cakes, roasted grain, and figs. She took five sheep that were ready to cook and a few bottles of wine. She loaded everything onto donkeys. Then she rode out to meet David. She didn't tell Nabal what she was doing. She left him at home eating and drinking with his friends.

Abigail bowed before David and asked for his kindness. She offered him the food she'd brought with her. Then she told David, "Please listen to me. Don't bother with Nabal. He is an evil and foolish man. Someday God will make you king. You do not want to be accused of killing innocent men because my husband was a fool."

David accepted Abigail's gift and her wisdom. He told her to return to her home in peace. David praised God for Abigail's advice.

The Jump to Jesus

Did you notice how kind and gentle Abigail was with David? God loves it when we are gentle with others. And the best person to teach us about how to be gentle with others is Jesus.

One of Jesus' disciples was called Peter. When Jesus was taken away to be put on the cross, Peter ran away and left him. Peter let Jesus down. When Jesus came back to life, he went to talk with Peter. Now do you think Jesus would be angry with Peter or gentle? Let's find out.

Jesus Gently Questions Peter
John 21

Jesus died and came to life again. Then he spent time with his disciples before he went back to heaven.

One evening, some of the disciples decided to go fishing. They fished all night without catching a thing.

When the sun came up, someone called from the shore, "Catch any fish?"

"None," they called back.

"Try tossing your net on the other side of the boat," called the stranger. And when they did, the net became so full of fish they could hardly drag it back into the boat.

Suddenly John realized who was on the beach. "It's Jesus!" he shouted. Then Peter dove into the sea and swam to shore. The others followed in the boat. When they all gathered on the shore, Jesus shared breakfast with them.

When breakfast was over, Jesus turned to Peter and asked, "Peter, do you love me?"

"Yes," said Peter. "You know I love you."

"Then feed my lambs," said Jesus. Again, he asked Peter, "Do you really love me?"

"Yes, Lord," said Peter. "You know that I love you."

"Then take care of my sheep," said Jesus. And for a third time, Jesus asked him gently, "Peter, do you love me?"

Peter felt bad because Jesus had asked him this question three times. Peter said sadly, "Lord, you know everything; you must know that I love you."

"Then feed my sheep," said Jesus.

THE
JESUS ANSWER

Did you guess that Jesus would be gentle with Peter? Jesus was calm and thoughtful with him. After that day, Peter spent every day of his life being a wonderful disciple for Jesus.

So how can you be thoughtful and considerate to others? Do what Jesus did. Be gentle in the words you say and the kind things you do. Always think about others. If you can do that, you will be a wonderful disciple for Jesus too.

Believe!

❊

KEY IDEA:
I am thoughtful, considerate, and calm with others.

KEY VERSE:

Let everyone know how gentle you are.

—*Philippians 4:5*

CHAPTER 30

Humility

BE

The Key Question:
What does it mean to value others before myself?

Have you ever met someone who thought they were better than everyone else? Maybe you've heard someone brag about how good they are? People like that are very proud of themselves. They think they are wonderful. But God does not want us to be proud people. God wants us to be humble people. Humble people don't think they're better than others. They don't show off, or think they're smarter than their friends. In fact, humble people think more highly of others than themselves. They value others more. A humble attitude pleases God.

A long time ago, King Nebuchadnezzar was king over the biggest country in the world. It made him very proud. He thought he was wonderful. Let's find out how God changed him from a proud king into a humble king.

God Humbles a Proud King
Daniel 4:1–37

King Nebuchadnezzar was king over the largest country in the world. He was a proud man. He believed all his power and success was because of his own work. One night, he had a bad dream. In his dream he saw a big, strong tree that touched the sky. The tree had beautiful leaves and lots of fruit. Animals slept under it and birds made nests in the branches. The tree could be seen from anywhere. Then a messenger came from heaven and said, "Cut down the tree. Let the animals run away and the birds fly off. Leave the stump and roots in the field. King Nebuchadnezzar will no longer think like a man. For seven years he will think and live like an animal. Then everyone will know that all power belongs to God. The Most High God is King."

King Nebuchadnezzar called his advisors together. He asked them what the dream meant. No one knew.

So he asked Daniel. God helped Daniel understand the dream. Daniel said to the king, "The dream is about you. The tall tree that was cut down means you will lose your power. You will eat and act like an animal for seven years. God wants you to know that the only real power is given through God. The remaining stump and roots mean that you will return to power and get your kingdom back. But first you must be humble and know that God is the King of heaven and earth. The dream is a warning. You must change. You must stop being evil and be kind to others. Then maybe this won't happen."

King Nebuchadnezzar didn't listen to the warning of the dream. One day, while the king boasted of his power, the dream came true. For seven years, the king acted and ate like an animal. At the end of the seven years, the king looked up at heaven. He announced there was only one true God. When King Nebuchadnezzar praised God and honored God's name, he became a better king than he had been before.

The Jump to Jesus

Can you imagine how King Nebuchadnezzar felt when he lived like an animal for seven long years? It must have been terrible. But did you see what happened? At the end of that time, the king changed from being proud to being humble.

Did you know that Jesus was a king too? But Jesus was very different from Nebuchadnezzar. Jesus could have been proud about being God's Son. Jesus could easily have boasted. But he never did. Jesus, the King of the whole world, was not born in a big, shiny palace. Jesus was born in a small, humble stable. Jesus, the most important man who ever walked on the earth, could have lived in the finest home, but Jesus had no home to call his own. And in one of the most amazing stories in the Bible, Jesus did something for his disciples that no proud person would ever do.

Jesus Humbles Himself in Front of His Disciples
John 13:1–17

A few days before Jesus died, he and his disciples ate supper together to celebrate the Feast of Passover. Jesus knew that his time on earth was almost over. He wanted his disciples to know how much he loved them. Before they started to eat, Jesus got up from the table. He poured water into a bowl and knelt down in front of Peter. Jesus began to wash Peter's dirty feet. Peter was confused. He didn't understand why Jesus was kneeling to do the humble job of a servant.

"No!" said Peter. "You can't wash my feet."

"If I don't, you are not part of me," explained Jesus.

"Oh," said Peter. "Then wash all of me!"

"Only your feet need to be washed," said Jesus as he continued washing. "You see, a person who has already bathed is clean, but his feet get dirty when he walks along the road." After Jesus washed all the disciples' feet, he sat back down at the supper table.

"Do you know why I did that?" he asked his disciples. "You call me Lord, and that is right. But today I gave you something to remember. A servant is not more important than his master. See how I served you? I want you to serve each other in the same way. And if you do these things, you will be blessed."

THE JESUS ANSWER

What a wonderful way for Jesus to show his disciples how much he loved them. Jesus, the King, was willing to become a servant and kneel before his friends to wash their dirty feet. Now if Jesus could be so humble and loving, don't you think we should be like that too? Learn from Jesus.

Be humble in all you do. Love others. Value them more than you value yourself. If you can do these things, then just like the disciples long ago, you will be blessed too.

Believe!

KEY IDEA:

I choose to value others more than myself.

KEY VERSE:

Think of others as better than yourselves.

—Philippians 2:3

You have just finished reading Bible stories about real people who lived long, long ago. They knew the one true God and were invited to take part in God's wonderful love story. In Bible times, many people believed in God, many did not. But for all of them, life was a journey.

Right now, Jesus invites *you* on a journey with him. Jesus invites you to *believe*—to believe in him, and to believe his Words to you in the Bible. As you think about the stories you have heard, be honest about your feelings. What stories were hard to believe? What things did you not understand? What else do you want to know about Jesus? Don't be afraid to ask these questions; talk about them with your parents. Pray to Jesus; ask him to help you find the answers. You're his precious child. As you talk to Jesus, he will whisper truth into your heart.

The more you believe, the more Jesus can change you from the inside out to become the very best person you can be. The more you believe in Jesus, the more you will be filled with love, joy, peace, patience, kindness, goodness, faithfulness, gentleness, and self-control. And when your life is filled with these things, everyone around you will see them.

As you grow up, try to *think* like Jesus. Try to *act* like Jesus. He will help you every day to *become* like Jesus. There's no better way to live. So BELIEVE.